BITTER
THISTLE,
SWEET
ROSE

BITTER THISTLE, SWEET ROSE

RUTH GLOVER

Beacon Hill Press of Kansas City
Kansas City, Missouri

3/13/95 Baker + Taylor 9.95

10   9   8   7   6   5   4   3   2   1

For my children—my friends:
Jeff, Holly, and Lynn

ABOUT THE AUTHOR

The fascinating bush country of central Saskatchewan is again the setting for Ruth Vogt Glover's second frontier romance novel. The area was especially significant for her first novel, *The Shining Light*, in which Mrs. Glover used her aunt's home in the Donnybrook school district, near Prince Albert, as the setting for main character Abbie Rooney's home. Though not living in the same dwelling, Mrs. Glover's aunt (her father's sister) still lives in the area, along with a number of the author's cousins.

Such firsthand descriptions apply as well to *Bitter Thistle, Sweet Rose*, in which the author incorporates more of her vivid memories of the area. Mrs. Glover grew up there in the 1920s and 1930s—yet life at that time in the Donnybrook school district was still virtually the same as it was in the turn-of-the-century setting of her novels.

"All during the time I was being raised we still carried in water, carried out the wash water, raised much of our food, used oil lamps, and traveled to town by horse and buggy," she comments. "Even after cars came to the area, they were not used in the winter; roads were just not open, so we used sleighs, toboggans, and other means of transportation."

After moving to Vancouver, Washington, in her teens and later marrying Hal Glover, the two went back for a visit in the late 1940s. "They were just getting electricity then—and the community was only three miles from the main highway," she notes. "About the only major changes up to that time were in fashions, since catalogs were relied on quite extensively."

Mrs. Glover has contributed over 300 articles, 575 poems, and 50 stories to a wide variety of Christian periodicals throughout the years. She and her husband currently live in The Dalles, Oregon, where Rev. Glover pastors a church while his wife pursues her love of writing. The couple have three children and seven grandchildren.

1

CAREFULLY, VERY CAREFULLY INDEED, LINN Graham lowered the battered zinc pail into the dark, icy depths of the well. In it she had placed supper's remains: butter sure to turn rancid if left near the range's warmth overnight, cream for the morning's porridge, cottage cheese of her own making, and enough fried chicken for dinner tomorrow noon following church.

Her concentration was challenged by a somewhat worn and worried mother hen and her rambunctious late-summer brood. Hopping on and off Linn's feet, spreading unformed wings, the noisy family fluttered and cheeped and scrambled for preferred positions near their food supplier.

"Biddy, Biddy!" Linn scolded mildly, concentrating on the descending pail and the chaos that would prevail if it were to dump its contents into the pure well water below. "You should teach your children better manners. Your days of freedom are coming to an end—tomorrow you go into the pen with the others. Life is not all tea and crumpets, you know!"

Nevertheless, with the bush's fragrance heavy and familiar in the late afternoon warmth of the autumn day, the week's tasks almost completed, and a rare free evening just ahead, life was good.

Vying with the hysterical cacophony at Linn's feet, her brother, Judd, called from the low doorway of the small log barn.

"I'm almost done here. Is there warm water for a bath?"

Linn nodded, uncertain of making herself heard over the barnyard ruckus, and Judd disappeared.

Leaning over the mouth of the well, Linn swung the pail at the end of the rope until it settled safely on the shelf a few feet above the water level.

On her return trip to the house, Linn tussled a tub from the granary into the lean-to kitchen and dipped water from the stove's reservoir for her brother's bath.

"I'll strain it," she said as Judd set the brimming pail of milk onto the kitchen table. "You go get your clean clothes."

Her heart went out to her brother; he worked so hard and so cheerfully. He deserved a little fun, and she hoped his first date with Modesty Trimble would go well after months of casting what their mother called "calf's eyes" in her direction.

Only now had Dolly Trimble slackened the reins on her eldest child.

"Kinda makes you wonder just what sort of girl she was herself," Judd had wondered darkly, "for her to distrust her girls like she does."

The milk was strained and the cheesecloth and the pail washed in sudsy water and rinsed when Judd returned. Stripped of his faded shirt, his young body was as brown as wheat bread from his sunburnt ear to his slim waist, where a narrow band of flesh gleamed, white as flour from the finest grist.

Before she turned her back to allow Judd to disrobe and slip into the tub, quick tears filled Linn's eyes. That slim figure seemed, suddenly, so vulnerable, so young, so . . . gallant!

"How Judd would scoff!" Linn thought ruefully, wringing out the dishrag one final time and tossing her brother a scrap of perfumed soap from the cupboard.

"Get rid of that barnyard smell," she teased lightly, "for Modesty's sake! Or will you get close enough for her to notice?"

"Not too close, I guess," Judd admitted, somewhat sheepishly. "If her mother so much as catches one hair on Modesty's head out of place, I can kiss her good-bye." Catching her sister's amused eye, he added plaintively, "And I haven't even kissed her at all."

In a day and a time bounded by many conventions, when the influence of old Queen Victoria pervaded even the backwoods of remote areas, Dolly Trimble's rigid rules were considered to be beyond reason. True, Charity, the second daughter, had trouble falling into the "little lady" category; but Modesty was all that her name implied. Her mother's warnings would be part and parcel of Judd's evening. Even so, he was obviously celebrating what was to him a victory.

"First time Modesty's been out with a man," he said, doubling himself into the tub while his sister turned her back discreetly.

"A man!" Linn mocked and ducked when Judd dipped a finger in the tub and flicked water toward her.

Linn tossed a worn, snowy towel toward him and went to get herself ready for the social.

When Judd had driven off in the spanking-clean buggy, waving a jaunty hand to his mother and sister watching from a window, Celia Graham turned to the rocking chair at the side of the cast-iron heater and the small fire flickering behind the isinglass window.

"Take a wrap, Linnie," she cautioned her daughter. "It looks like rain. Perhaps you should take the lantern. . . ."

"I could walk it blindfolded," Linn scoffed. "Don't worry about me, Mum. I'll be fine."

Linn kissed her mother's thin face, glanced into the mirror over the buffet at the mossy eyes gazing back at her and the sun-streaked, tumbled hair, and took a bulky sweater from the row of nails behind the kitchen door. She then slipped out into the deepening twilight. In a matter of minutes she had crossed the yard, skirted the nearby schoolyard, and reached the road.

Overhead, the loon's cry wavering from a nearby slough mingled unmusically with the distant sound of Canada geese as they turned southward, calling a final farewell to forest lands and flowing waters. At her side, the underbrush rustled with the passing of some night creature.

Linn's slim legs moved along the familiar track with a light step not far removed from childhood. Young womanhood sat gracefully upon her, and the proud head was lifted as if in anticipation of life itself. She strode out briskly; weariness from the day's work wasn't evident now, but only an expectation of what the evening would hold.

Perhaps the chief attraction of the social—eclipsing the pleasure of meeting friends not seen often during the busy summer—was the break it offered in the season's dawn-to-dark workload. The harvest, from field and meadow and garden and bush, took precedence over everything else, for young people and children as well as adults; their very existence depended on it. But tonight restless minds and exuberant spirits were bringing bone-weary bodies from the surrounding homesteads like mice from a razed haymow. The narrow roads were thronged with Linn's friends and acquaintances hurrying, as she was, to the refreshment of a few hours stolen from the drudgery of work and the necessity of sleep.

And for all of them a lantern was certainly unnecessary, except on the blackest of nights. To have strayed from the road would have been difficult to do; brush pressed close on each side. Just beyond, a vigorous stand of poplars and birches and willows tossed thinning leaves. And through it all—tangled endlessly across this fertile parkland between the branches of the Saskatchewan River—hazel and saskatoon, pin cherry and gooseberry, chokeberry and raspberry battled for room.

Bush, they called it. Many people were intimidated by it. It crowded the roads, circled the fields; farmyards were small islands in its green sea. And it was redolent with its own distinctive scent: grass, grain, dried berries, and leaf mold, washed by frequent rains. Tonight a small wind carried with it the smell of newly harvested fields and sun-baked straw. Linn breathed it and found it no different than she had known for 18 years.

Lamplight through stiff lace curtains beckoned from the windows of the two-story log parsonage. Linn threaded her way expertly through rigs tied to the encircling fence and stepped up to the porch. Elva Victor, ever alert to her duties as pastor's wife, hovered at the door.

"Linn?" Mrs. Victor swung the door wide and looked beyond the young woman to the shadows of the yard. "Didn't Judd come?"

"He's pulling in now."

"Why—who's that with him?"

Linn smiled at the little lady's attempt to hide her curiosity with decorum and whispered conspiratorially, "Modesty."

"Modesty!" Mrs. Victor stifled a gasp.

Like everyone else in Wildrose, the minister's wife knew that Dolly Trimble rode herd on her two maturing daughters as diligently as though she were corralling a pair of prize fillies—too much so, most people agreed, because Charity, at least, seemed to be rebelling. Even now Linn heard a shriek that could be coming only from that bumptious 16-year-old.

"Apparently Dolly isn't here," Linn remarked dryly.

"Good heavens, no! And I really must get back!" Elva

Victor hurried inside, a worried frown creasing her plump features, caused, no doubt, by her responsibility as chaperon to the daughter of that pious, rigid member of her husband's flock—Dolly Trimble.

Linn was greeted warmly, and she watched in amusement as Judd and Modesty entered to the sly grins, hoots, and whistles of their friends. Charity, greeting the young couple boisterously, subsided under the quelling look of her more mature sister. But there was jealousy in Charity's eyes, Linn thought, although mixed with approval. The sisters, separated in age by less than two years, had been close all their lives. In everything. Until now.

Marc Szarvas moved to Linn's side. "What do you know?" he said admiringly, his eyes on Judd. "He actually pulled it off!"

"And don't you wish *you* could?" Linn watched Marc's eyes stray toward the frolicsome Charity.

Marc's square jaw tightened. "Her mother would never allow it. And," he added somewhat bitterly, "not just because of Charity's age."

Linn's hand touched her friend's arm sympathetically. As well known as Dolly's firm hand on her girls' lives was her belligerence toward the immigrants that continued to infiltrate the back country, willing to take up land overlooked by others. Hardworking, honorable, but—different. That the country was built on immigrants never seemed to cross Dolly's mind. "French—of course," she was known to say, "and English and Scotch. But these jabbering foreigners . . . !"

"Somebody better snatch that girl up quick—for her own good!" Marc continued as he watched Charity through narrowed eyes. "Does Dolly ever think of that?" And Marc spent the evening teasing Charity until that young lady was almost dizzy with embarrassment and pleasure.

But it was more or less the usual end-of-summer gathering until two strangers were ushered in. Linn decided they were the Farley cousins, new arrivals in Wildrose.

These two didn't fit the assembled group and didn't stay long. "I wonder what they thought they were coming to," Linn thought with amusement as she glanced around at the bright, mostly young faces. One thing was certain: the newcomers were men, not boys.

"I want all of you to meet Trapper and Boyd Farley," the minister's wife was saying after motioning for attention. "Brother Victor (she always called her husband that in public) met them last week and urged them to come and get acquainted. As you know, they have taken over the Cooley homestead."

The group quieted. Elva Victor turned her bright, bird-like eyes on the two tall men. "Your nearest neighbors," she said, moving toward Linn, "are the Grahams. This is Linnet Graham. And this," indicating Judd, "is her brother, Judd, with Modesty Trimble." Moving on, she pointed out, "And this is Charity, Modesty's sister. . . ." Charity, Linn noted with disbelief, batted her eyes at the pair with atrocious audacity.

The newcomers moved around the room, towering over the neat figure of the minister's wife, nodding politely and shaking the hands that were proffered to them. They spoke quietly and moved easily with an air of restraint. But Linn had the feeling that beneath that control lay powerful strengths—physical and emotional.

Trapper and Boyd Farley, men of wide shoulders and strong backs and dark good looks, were very much alike. For they were not only cousins, but double cousins. Trapper was taller, Linn thought, or was it Boyd? Boyd appeared to be heavier and a little broader than his cousin "Trapp," as he was explaining he preferred to be called. "It's a family name," he said, "and, yes, it is what Boyd and I did in the north: trapping and fishing."

Strangers were always of interest, and these were

more interesting than most, Linn decided, with a small inner smile at her frank appraisal of their masculinity and magnetism. That others were equally affected was apparent from the simpers and glances—mostly shy—with which the young women of the group responded to the introductions.

Abbie Jameson, helping to chaperon the party, thrust a cup of hot cocoa into Linn's hand and followed Linn's eyes across the room to the straight back and strong shoulders of Trapper Farley. At that moment—as though aware of her eyes on him—Trapper Farley turned his head, and his gaze (darkly blue, Linn thought in that heart-stopping instant) fixed on hers. One second . . . two seconds . . . and Linn's cup tipped in her hand. A grin touched the man's mouth fleetingly.

With an obvious start, Linn dropped her eyes from that hypnotic contact and furious flushing (hating herself for it) and swiped at the stain dampening her skirt.

"Not your run-of-the-mill men, would you say?" Abbie asked mischievously.

Abbie, a new bride herself, obviously recognized and appreciated the attractions of the Farley cousins. But across the room Jamie, her husband, a willing helper of the social along with Abbie, was Abbie's heart's choice. Even now his eyes met hers across the heads of the young people in between, and Linn saw and appreciated the color that warmed Abbie's face and the glow that lit her amber eyes.

All of Wildrose had celebrated the joyous love that eventually blossomed and brought healing to two who were alone and lonely after the deaths of their mates. Now Abbie's children—twins Corcoran and Cameron and their sister, small Merry—were playing upstairs with the Victor children. And Abbie was flushing like any new wife under her husband's warm gaze.

Abbie turned her attention back to Linn and the newcomers, Trapper and Boyd Farley. "They're both single, I understand, Linn," she teased.

"And likely to stay that way, if it depends on me," answered Linn, a trifle more tartly than was called for. "They're not my type."

Just what was her type, Linn wasn't sure. But her eyes moved across the room until they alighted on another dark head set on strong, young shoulders, though not as rugged perhaps as those of the man whose gaze had left such a flutter in her breast.

Abram Weatherby raised his head at that moment and caught Linn's eye. She looked away quickly, chagrined at being caught in still another indiscretion. And her mossy eyes glittered as she laid the blame for both of them at the feet planted so firmly on the end of the long legs of the man called Trapper Farley.

2

STANDING CASUALLY AT THE EDGE OF THE group in the sturdy rural parsonage, Trapper and Boyd Farley ate the sandwiches and tarts and drank the coffee pressed on them by the minister's wife. And then with a grace unexpected in men so rugged, they bade her goodnight and turned to go, explaining, "It's been a busy week."

"Probably glad to get out of here," Linn thought with a sniff. Blindman's buff couldn't be very stimulating for these northwoodsmen.

Trapper Farley's eyes definitely sought Linn's as he passed her. Determined not to reveal her mortification over her slopped drink, Linn, chin lifted, met the blue gaze levelly in spite of her vexation at the warm blood flooding her cheeks. Trapper's dark head dipped politely in her direction, and Linn's smarting ego immediately suspected it hid a wicked grin. And when the door closed on what her inflamed imagination interpreted as a mocking lift to his handsome lips, Linn's eyes blazed, and she turned away abruptly to catch once more the narrow gaze of Abram Weatherby.

As Linn put on her sweater and prepared to leave at the close of the evening's activities, a hand touched her elbow. "Want a ride?"

Abram had made his way across the crowded room and was looking down at her with a small smile. Surprised, Linn raised her eyes to his blue ones (though not darkly blue) and tried to speak casually. "Thanks. I'd appreciate it. Of course, Judd isn't going straight home."

"I can see why not," Abram said. "But it looks like rain. You don't want to get your feet soaked."

True, it did look like it was going to rain. But never before had Abram expressed a concern for her welfare.

Abram Weatherby was five or six years older than Linn. Although she had known him—or, better said, known *of* him—across the years, it had never been on familiar terms. For one thing, he was not in Judd's circle of close friends.

Abram had been raised in the adjoining community of Cloud and had recently moved to Wildrose to farm his own place, previously homesteaded but left undeveloped by some relative. It was rumored that he attended the "shindigs" in the Sandhill area on the edge of the Saskatchewan River, an undesirable atmosphere for church-raised Wildrose youth and frowned on by most parents. Too often the foot-stomping dances were made wilder still—and not a few fights resulted—from the "home brew" that invariably made its appearance. There was an unknown quality about Abram; perhaps it was because he wasn't as yet thoroughly known by the community. Looking up into those blue eyes, Linn couldn't imagine the man to be any different from the boys with whom she had grown up.

Linn had done her share of dreaming about Abram Weatherby, but she knew a half-dozen girls who did the same. He was doing well on his farm, and it was the opinion of mothers and daughters alike that whoever got Abram Weatherby would get a catch. Many a young man had been tamed by the right marriage.

So when he spoke to her now—casually, it was true, but with something in his eyes—Linn's heart quickened. Recovering her good sense hastily, she recognized that he was, after all, going her way. And it was indeed spitting rain, according to the comments of those preceding them into the night; any thoughtful person would offer a neighbor a ride.

"Will we see you tomorrow?" asked the minister's wife at the door. It was both a question and a reminder, for the next day was Sunday and meeting time. The little lady's face was concerned under neatly bunned hair.

"You can't blame her," thought Linn kindly. "It's her husband's job and their whole reason for being here." And it was true; the Victors were unstinting in their service. They married the community's young, visited their sick, baptized their believers, and were central to much that went on in the community. Preacher, teacher—the two people of any rural region whose influence touched more lives than anyone else's; one had to appreciate them.

Linn recalled Brother Victor's support at the time of her father's death two years previously and his present concern for her mother's failing health, and responded, "Yes, of course—I'll see you in the morning," while Abram nodded.

It was the usual schedule. Human contact—it was important to all, and Sunday services offered the only regular opportunity. To see your neighbor, conduct a little business, catch up on the local news, and do a bit of courting were as much reasons for meeting together as for worshiping God—more so, to some. Bush people, whether church people or not, closed down operations on Sunday, and plows and harrows and seeders and rakes sat idle. The day of rest was an oasis in a weary week to all "that labour and are heavy laden."

So Linn gave her ready assurance, added her thanks for the party, and stepped beyond the circle of lamplight.

Silver drops were spattering the night with a touch of magic as she climbed with the agility of youth and long practice into the buggy, and Abram untied the horse; soon it increased until it was a sifting rain. Linn drew her sweater, an inadequate protection, more tightly about her.

It was then Abram shifted both reins into one hand and put the free arm around her. It was such a sensible thing to do . . . kind, really . . . that Linn submitted to it naturally.

Being extremely pretty—with her tangled mop of streaky-colored hair, pert nose, eyes the unfathomable shade of a deep, shadowed pool, and her slim, graceful figure—Linn had experienced numerous pleasant encounters with eager young men. But never before had she permitted an embrace. Now, in view of the night's chill, it hardly seemed reasonable to make an issue of the hand that pulled her close.

"Little Linnet," Abram murmured over the muted thud of the horse's hooves, "you've grown up."

"You noticed!" she responded banteringly, but her breath caught in her throat in a strange way.

"I notice," he said seriously, and his arm tightened.

Linn looked up at the face so close to hers, glinting with rain . . . and something more? How silly to assume it! It was absurd in the extreme to confuse a brotherly gesture with . . . something more. But just the same, Linn couldn't resist enjoying the experience.

It seemed incredible, come to think of it. She, Linnet Graham, with Abram Weatherby's arm around her! And if a momentary remembrance of a mocking smile and darkly blue eyes flashed into her thoughts, it only served to open her mind—and her heart—to the present reality.

The night vibrated with new feelings. For wasn't Abram murmuring things she had never heard before? Sweet, foolish words? Urgent, compelling words? And didn't his lips touch her rain-spangled hair lightly from time to time? The spring-seated buggy rocked through the night and seemed to Linn a fairy boat adrift in some misty sea.

When Abram stopped the rig at the dark schoolhouse, offered his hand and drew her with soft eyes and firm fingers, she stepped down with only the briefest hesitation and walked with him, as though in a dream, into the empty building.

Faint light fell through the tall, narrow windows of the schoolroom into the entrance area with its surrounding hooks and bounded with wide benches; enough light for Abram to reach unerringly for Linn and with an urgency that sent an unexpected thrill through her entire being.

The drumming rain played a hypnotic accompaniment to the symphony that swelled soundlessly in the pulsating darkness. In a silence touched by magic, Linn's heart, generous in its innocency, opened like a spring blossom unfolds to the summer sun.

Her response was joyous and spontaneous. For wasn't Abram once again whispering sweet promises? And didn't her young heart respond warmly and willingly?

Linn's heart danced in rhythm with the shining motes adrift in the shaft of moonlight. Of this once-in-a-lifetime moment she had dreamed; for this precious moment she had kept herself. With a heart previously untouched, Linn gave herself to the lovely moment gladly and fully.

But Abram's ardor bordered on the possessive. How could he know that the very walls of this small school-church building were saturated with the teaching and training, the preaching and praying, of years? Here Linn's grandparents had worshiped, pouring their love and sacrifice into the rustic sanctuary erected on a corner of the homestead. Here her mother and father had dedicated her and pledged to raise her according to godly precepts. Here she had heard the gospel message every Sunday of her life.

Now, in the midst of whirling thoughts and heart full of tumultuous feelings, prudence and discretion prevailed. There was, after all, tomorrow, and tomorrow, and tomorrow . . .

"Abram . . . ," she managed, against the insistent lips seeking her own. And "Abram!" she said urgently when he seemed not to hear and certainly not to heed, and made an effort to disengage herself from his demanding arms.

Dizzy with new feelings, she tried to explain. "There's all of life ahead for us," she whispered, and added shyly, "darling."

Those warm moments and the lovely expectancy of sweeter times to come carried Linn from Abram's reluctantly loosed embrace to the buggy and across a silent ride home. Nor did they dim when Abram deposited her at her door with a brief good-bye.

Linn watched as Abram slapped the reins of the horse's rump and careened out of the yard, and she whispered, "Tomorrow . . ."

 3

SWAYING WITH PRACTICED GRACE TO THE jolting of the train, the conductor waited.

Kate Mason's attention was riveted on the scenery flashing past—mile upon endless mile of prairie, with here and there a field stretching to the horizon, golden with fresh-cut stubble, and with much land still unclaimed or perhaps just not yet under cultivation.

It was familiar to the young woman who had been born in this heartland of the grain belt, but its immensity filled her with astonishment. For the moment, it made her forget her last glimpse of her family as they waved bravely from the station, a station, she could see now, that was well-nigh lost in the midst of this awesome land.

The conductor pulled a watch from his fob pocket, studied it, put it back, stretched forth a hand, and, finally, cleared his throat.

With a start, Kate lifted her eyes, aware that her velvetta hat had slipped because of the jouncing she endured as she had been absorbed with the scene from the train window and that the cherished black silk pompons in its braid were trembling over her left eye. Aware of her new need for dignity, Kate straightened the modest creation.

"Oh, I'm sorry!" she said quickly, and loosened the strings of the bag she had been clutching on her lap, fumbling among its contents.

"No hurry, I'm sure," the man said patiently. He took the ticket she proffered, looked at her with mild curiosity, and asked, "Teacher?"

"How did you know?" Kate asked, surprised.

"Pshaw! You get so you can tell. Back there," and his head bobbed toward the rear of the coach, "are two more. Going to La Ronge."

Kate craned to catch a glimpse of the fortunate women. "That's where I wanted to go!" she exclaimed in a voice tinged with envy. "Flin Flon . . . Pelican Narrows . . . Cree Lake. . . ." Dreams dreamed and reluctantly put aside, her tone indicated.

The walrus-mustached man studied the ticket in his hand. "Meridian," he read aloud. "Not north, of course, but not south either. A sort of in-between place, I guess you could say. The park strip, some call it. Bush country, you know."

"I know," she sighed.

Kate's mother's lips had tightened with apprehension when her daughter expressed her desire to be part of the educational system of the vast Northwest. And she had sighed with relief when arrangements were finalized for a school not unrealistically far from her prairie home. But Kate's disappointment with the "in-between" place was obvious. It had definitely been a second choice.

Preparing to teach, she had been teased enough about the known fact: An assignment to a community school was a guarantee of marriage. Countless homes across the territory boasted a former teacher as wife and mother.

But finding a husband had been the least of Kate's considerations. To be a devoted teacher, helping change the course of her country's history—that had been the factor that had motivated her. And to do it where education, at the present time, was the poorest had been her goal. The "far north" beckoned.

But she had received, and finally accepted, a position to an "in-between" place. The conductor had confirmed it.

"Actually," she said, sighing again, "I'm going to the Wildrose School. Meridian is the train stop."

"Know it well," the man said, adding with a grin, "what there is of it, such as it is. Train only goes about 20 miles farther, to Prince Albert. Too bad you're not going there . . ."

Sighing again, Kate turned to the window once more, only to have her sighs hushed abruptly.

While they had talked, the miles, clacking away quickly, had taken with them the unbroken stretches of the unending prairie, and now, stretching across her vision from horizon to horizon, the green and shaggy bush raised its head. Briefly Kate had the sensation that the train stood still and the living wall rushed to meet her; within moments it swirled around her.

Just that dramatically the vast plains she had called home were left behind, and she was caught up in the leafy welcome of the bushland.

When the train stopped at Meridian, Kate felt enfolded in the luxuriant embrace of the bush.

Straining like a dog on a leash, the train paused only long enough for Kate's luggage and a few boxes, sacks, and crates to be unloaded, and then the whistle shrieked into the clear, crisp air and the puffing monster lurched forward, gathering speed for its run into Prince Albert.

"Miss Mason?"

As outlined by letter, a school board member was there to meet her. "John Edwards," he said.

The man's fine, intelligent face, browned by the summer sun, was creased in a cordial smile. He directed Kate toward a buggy, and with a courtesy that was somehow unexpected in this backwoods area, helped her to the iron step and up into the rig. Not an experienced judge of character, Kate's favorable opinion of the man was instinctive and, she was to conclude later on, a good one.

The buggy tipped as John Edwards took his place beside her and picked up reins shiny with age and use. "His hands," Kate thought fleetingly, "are better shaped for a scholar's pen than for a farmer's plow." But they were capable, and with a slap of the reins and a command given in a clear-timbred voice, they were off.

Crossing the road—a dusty ribbon tying the entire area to Prince Albert—they slipped into a narrow opening in the trees. Almost immediately the station, false-fronted store, blacksmith shop, post office, and two towering granaries disappeared from sight.

With granaries Kate was well familiar; their massive bulks dominated the prairies where she had been born and raised and were an emblem of the life that existed across the ever-expanding grain belt.

"So far, so good," she murmured. At John Edwards' turn of the head, she asked hastily, "Do we have far to go?"

"About five miles. The district of Wildrose lies beyond the Meridian School District. Schools here are close together so children won't have great distances to go. It's killing-cold most of the school year. But I guess you know about cold."

Kate knew about cold. The prairies were often desperately cold. Surely the bush would offer some protection from blizzard winds that swept the open prairie so mercilessly from time to time. Now late flowers bloomed and birds flashed around the rig as they passed, and only the chill of the oncoming evening hinted at the bitter weather soon to be upon them.

"Wildrose," she ventured. "I know it's located between the branches of the Saskatchewan River."

"Sisiskatchewan, the Indians call it. It flows from the Rocky Mountains, of course, to Lake Winnipeg, and it quite naturally splices the Shield to the north and the prairies of the south." John Edwards sounded like a teacher himself, rather than a bush man—or, with his richly modulated voice, a professor.

"Now here," John said, "Wildrose district begins." And with interesting and informative comments he introduced the newcomer to the homesteads they were passing, and their occupants. Here and there the bush had been slashed and chopped away and a cabin erected. At one such yard John waved to a slim, young woman, who turned her head at the sound of the passing buggy. At her side danced a small girl, and behind her surged a stream of chickens intent on the pail in her hand.

It was obvious that no passerby was ignored in the seclusion of the bush country. Curiosity and loneliness caused people to turn and look; friendliness and a need for human contact, however small, prompted a wave and a greeting.

The woman paused to wave, and the chickens plowed into her heels to scatter, squawking, and form ranks again, wings lifted, legs churning, greedy eyes beady, as the parade resumed its march across the clearing.

Soon John gestured toward what appeared to be one of the more prosperous farms in the area. Fields spread around a tall, narrow, unpainted frame house, log barn, and several outbuildings.

"Home," John said briefly.

Quickening its pace, the horse turned in at the gate automatically, obviously "home."

To enter a bush country home through any but the kitchen door was to be branded a rank stranger, not only to the inhabitants but to the culture of the area. Certainly the horse knew the custom and pulled to the rear of the house and stopped at the small porch with its protective overhang. From the shadows stepped John's wife. Her first smile was for John.

The woman's greeting put to rest all the uncertainties

Kate had been feeling about the place where she was to board: "Welcome to Wildrose, Miss Mason," and her second smile was as genuine as her first. The hand she extended to help the younger woman from the buggy was warm, and her grip was firm. Holding open the screen door, she ushered the new member of the household into a kitchen where supper's fragrance added its own amen.

Kate's glance took in the cat curled on a rag rug at the side of the shining range, the spice cake cooling on the sideboard, and, in the room beyond, a table covered with a white cloth and set for four.

"John will unhitch and put the horse away," Maggie Edwards said as she took Kate's bag from her husband's hand. "I'll take you on up to your room."

The graceful woman led the way into a narrow hall and up a steep flight of stairs. From the upper landing two doors opened. Continuing to the second room, Maggie entered and set Kate's luggage on the bed's white coverlet.

"This is wonderful, Mrs. Edwards!" Kate exclaimed, pleased by the brightness and cleanliness of the small room. "I'll be just fine here. Thanks so much—"

"Call me 'Maggie.' And if you don't mind, we'll call you by your first name. Kathleen, isn't it?"

"Kate."

"You'll get 'Miss Mason' most of the time, I'm afraid. Comes with the job. Be thankful it isn't '*Sister*,' which is what the preacher's wife has to put up with! 'Kate' it will be."

Kate stifled an impulse to hug this new acquaintance who, with a few words and a kind smile, had put her at ease and erased many of her anxieties.

"There are extra blankets in the bottom bureau drawer," Maggie explained practically. "I think the water in the pitcher is warm, and there's always more in the reservoir on the range. Oh yes," she added, pointing to a small grate in the floor. "This should be open in the morning so that you can get some warmth from the kitchen. Days are still nice enough, but nights are getting cold." And Maggie Edwards smiled and returned to her work.

Kate stepped to the window, pulled back the flocked curtain, threw up the sash, and leaned out, breathing deeply of the distinctive aroma of the bush mingled with the more familiar odors of a farm.

A movement at the barn door caught her eye; from its shadows a man's face lifted toward her. But it wasn't John Edwards. A smaller man, Kate thought, as the figure emerged to lounge carelessly against the side of the door, to roll a cigarette, and do it with his eyes never wavering from his study of the girl in the window.

Hastily, Kate drew back and allowed the curtain to fall into place. When the man's face, even at this distance, twisted into a smile that Kate could think of only as sardonic and his shoulders shrugged arrogantly, she closed the window with unnecessary vigor.

"What have we here?" she fumed. "A rooster in the barnyard? And a bantam at that!"

In the dimming light she shook out her dresses, hung them in the clothes press, and laid the remaining items in the bureau drawers and on the lace-edged dresser scarf. A box would arrive soon with books, teaching materials, and personal items such as pictures, mementos of home, and winter clothes. Shoving the bag under the bed, Kate turned toward the stairs.

The door to the other bedroom, when she reached it, was open, revealing bright rugs, crisp curtains, and a spotless coverlet—a comfy, homey room.

Pausing, she noticed a small, oval, gold-framed picture of a child on the bedside table. Above the handsome face a curl swirled over the brow in a distinctive cowlick; the chin was deeply indented under lips unusually sweet for a boy.

"Not the man in the barn door—that's for sure," Kate concluded and made her way to the kitchen.

4

"MAY I HELP?" KATE ENTERED THE KITCHEN from the dark stairwell.

"Just sit on that stool by the range and relax," Maggie Edwards said. "You must be tired after a good part of the day on the train, not to mention the buggy ride from Meridian."

Kate sank gratefully onto the stool, familiar with all the last-minute touches her hostess was putting on the meal—slicing a roast of beef, turning to the range that was belching heat to thicken gravy, lifting fragrant buns from the warming oven.

"Mum and Rhoda will be doing the same things just about now," Kate thought with a small pang of homesickness.

But such thoughts were nipped in the bud when the door opened and John Edwards entered, accompanied by the "barn door" man.

"Miss Mason," John said, "this is Gabriel Goss. Gabe —Miss Mason, our new teacher."

The man's flat eyes had a curious, slumberous look to them; the expression on his smooth face was a continuation of the one he had lifted to her window. Even as he took her hand, the eyes held hers in a sort of hypnotic grip, much like, she thought briefly, a snake transfixes its prey. "Pleasure, I'm sure," he murmured.

31

Barely restraining, "The pleasure is all yours, I'm sure," Kate gave herself a mental shake, reproaching herself for her strange reaction.

Surely the man was no mind reader, but his strange eyes seemed to harden momentarily, and when she attempted to withdraw her hand, his fingers tightened.

Flushing, Kate realized that without an obvious pull her hand was not likely to be released soon. And—was it possible the man was fondling it? With John washing his hands at the washstand in the corner of the room and Maggie dipping water into the teakettle almost at Kate's elbow?

Quite clearly the impossible creature was pressing her hand in a blatantly suggestive manner! With an effort—the grip was surprisingly steely for such a slim man—Kate pulled her hand free.

Before she could stop herself, she wiped her palm on her skirt. Another quick flash in the narrow eyes told her the man had seen and understood her reaction.

Following Maggie to the dining room, Kate wondered if the man's gaze was fixed on her back and if his lips were curled in a smirk at her discomfort.

John bowed his head and said a blessing, and through it Kate's face crawled with a suspicion that Gabriel Goss's sleepy eyes were caressing her face as strangely as his hand had kneaded her hand.

When finally he turned his attention to the passing of the food, his rather small head, bent over his plate, revealed that his wispy, colorless hair was thinning. Fine lines around his pale eyes gave the lie to his deceptively youthful look. "Forty, if he's a day," Kate surmised, "but wants to be thought much younger."

Questioning her own senses regarding what had happened in the kitchen, or whether indeed it had, Kate gathered her wits about her and asked, "Are you a Wildrose man, Mr. Goss?"

She was not surprised to see something—anger, perhaps, or amusement—in his eyes momentarily. But his voice was silky when he said, "I'm the hired man. John hired me—and you."

There was nothing unusual about a farm having a hired man, but his answer had been calculated to unsettle her. Kate lowered her eyes before her anger could show; she had an idea it would have pleased him.

John looked up sharply and broke the uncomfortable silence with an outline of plans for the next week's work, and Maggie explained to Kate, "We have a small cabin out back that Gabe uses. Usually he gets his own meals there, but I invite him to eat with us on special occasions . . . like this." Maggie's smile was intended to put the newcomer at ease.

As Maggie rose to fill the teacups, the lamplight highlighted her forehead and the hair that fell to one side from an unusual cowlick. "Do you have children, Maggie?" Kate asked impulsively.

Maggie's hand jerked and the tea splashed. John's chair crashed to the floor as he leaped to his feet and hurried to his wife's side.

"I'm . . . I'm all right, John," Maggie murmured. "The pot just seemed to slip in my hand."

In the confusion of cleaning up, getting the food and dishes from the table, removing the cloth and setting it to soak, Kate's question went unanswered. The spice cake and fresh tea were served amid somewhat strained banalities.

When Maggie washed the dishes, Kate insisted on drying. "Gabe," Kate asked hesitantly, "—is he a local man?"

"John met him in P.A.—Prince Albert, that is. He had been working on a farm there but was looking for another place. He's . . . well, he's not very communicative, and we haven't pried. So I guess I have to say we don't know very much about him."

Kate made a deliberate effort to put the man—with his strange eyes and hands—behind her. Maggie, burying her head in a cabinet drawer, said in a muffled voice, "John and I have no children, Kate. Ah . . . here it is . . ." And she emerged with a fresh tablecloth.

Kate's response was cut off by the opening of the kitchen door and the entrance of Gabriel Goss, now dressed in well-pressed pants and a belted jacket over a fresh shirt. His hair had been oiled and combed smoothly against his neat head, an odor of bay rum surrounded him, and his hat was in his hand. And Kate knew instinctively that he had stopped by for her benefit.

"I'm off to the parsonage," he said to Maggie.

The parsonage! A bubble of laughter rose in Kate's throat and strangled her. Gabe glanced at her sharply. Kate coughed and managed to lift a straight face toward Maggie, who explained, "It's a social gathering. The Victors— our preacher and his wife—invited Gabe especially. All the young people will be there . . ."

The bubble threatened to erupt again.

"If you'd care to go . . . ," Gabe said smoothly.

"Oh, no! That is—I couldn't. Thank you, anyway." Kate's excuse was stumbling, which infuriated her and seemed to please Gabriel Goss.

"Ah, well," he murmured, "perhaps next time."

Putting his hat carefully on his head, the hired man bowed himself from the room as smoothly as though he were leaving the finest drawing room.

Maggie's face was thoughtful as she lit a lamp and handed it to Kate, who managed a "Goodnight—and thanks again, Maggie," as she headed for the stairwell.

In the upstairs hall the soft kerosene light fell through the open door of Maggie's and John's bedroom, giving a warm glow to the simple furnishings, muting bright colors, throwing shadows on the wall.

The moving circle lit the bedside table. Kate's steps faltered and her brows drew together in perplexity—the table was bare.

The little gold-framed picture was gone.

FROM THE BIRD'S-EYE VIEW OF THE WILD GEESE flying in ragged formation across the wide sky, the small building must have seemed a focal point. Here four roads met, and down them streamed an array of horse-drawn rigs: buggies, democrats, surreys, wagons. And around it, like a missionary society's crazy quilt, spread a patchwork of fields, bound with green, knotted with clusters of houses and barns, and stitched with neat rows of stubble.

The assembling group stepped gingerly over puddles left by the night's rain, greeted friends and neighbors, and commented without fail on the fine day and the fact that with any kind of luck the stooks, already steaming in the sunshine, would dry, and the harvest be completed. Luck, and the benevolence of a good God, a few added, clutching Bibles in hands that were stained, bruised, swollen, chapped, or grimed in direct accordance with the week's tasks.

Linnet Graham, lingering on the schoolhouse steps, her sun-streaked head lifted with scarcely veiled eagerness toward the south fork, wondered if her cheeks were too flushed and her eyes too bright and prayed that no one would notice. Her tense fingers worried a scrap of cambric; with a flash of insight she saw the discreet lace at its border as a small evidence of the prudence that had always hemmed her life.

And the small building behind her, both schoolhouse and church—into which she had stepped each Sunday of her life—was at the heart of it. But just as the delicate tatting raveled in her hand, so had, just a few short hours ago, her careful training been threatened with raveling. Now, in the morning sun, she marveled at the restraint that had surfaced and thanked God—and her mother's prayers—for it.

Linn's attention was diverted abruptly by the arrival of a wagon in which rode a stranger, the new schoolteacher, she supposed. Confirming it, Albin Trimble stepped from the watching crowd and loped to the side of the wagon, reaching a hand to help the newcomer down.

Rawboned, rednecked, and sunburned, Albin was ungainly in the stiff Sunday clothes his wife, Dolly, insisted he wear, befitting his status as a deacon of the church and a member of the school board. Dolly hovered close to her husband's shoulder, her sharp eyes scanning the new young woman critically.

"Even Dolly," Linn thought, "can't find fault with this one." For the teacher was modest and neat, with a pretty, open face.

With a dignity all his own, Albin Trimble introduced himself.

"And this," he said, nodding in the direction of the stout woman at his heels, "is my wife, Dolly." He motioned forward two young women and said with pride, "My daughters, Modesty and Charity. And over there," Albin pointed toward the swings, "is my youngest, Harmony."

Modesty and Charity smiled and murmured a greeting and turned with the newcomer to the schoolhouse. Charity was explaining, rather defensively, it seemed to Linn, who knew her well, "I'm still in school . . . I missed a year with rheumatics . . . this is my last year . . ."

And when the 16-year-old gave a provocative twitch

to her hips, Linn looked automatically for the reason. Sure enough, a man walked behind them.

Catching the girl's glance, a half-smile lifted a corner of the narrow lips on Gabriel Goss's smooth face. An older woman might have envied the self-confidence with which Charity turned and gurgled, "Hello! Remember me? From the social last night?"

"Ah, yes . . . Charity," the man replied, and his step quickened. And so did the step of Dolly. Soon she was in full sail behind her daughters.

Linn could only be glad that the attention of the group, who knew her every bit as well as she knew Charity, was focused on the little scenario and away from herself. For almost immediately a rider cantered into view over the crest of the south road, and her heart came into her throat.

Turning quickly, Linn fled into the building to mingle unobtrusively with the folks who were squeezing themselves into small desks and settling onto the benches at the sides of the room under tall, narrow windows.

Linn sank into a seat; her legs, usually so strong and lithe, were trembling, and her head was awhirl with vivid mental pictures of the events that had happened in this room the previous night: events that even now quickened her heart to a new and unfamiliar beat and turned her thoughts toward the man who had undoubtedly taken a seat in the rear, where, by custom, the unmarried men congregated.

She thanked God fervently that the walls couldn't speak, although she knew it was irreverent of her to do so.

Only a new shyness kept her from turning around and seeking Abram Weatherby's eyes. She was sure that if she did, his gaze would be on her, full of meaning. She shivered with the sheer delight of it, followed by a small and unexpected pang of guilt (she had, after all, been so unprincipled and daring!). Fumbling for her hankie, already tortured, she pulled free another length of thread.

"Let us rise."

Brother Victor's voice lifted above the hubbub. With a great heaving and clattering, the congregation rose from pinched positions, opening well-worn hymnals to the announced selection.

In spite of a suit grown shiny at the knees and seat and a shirt whose collar and cuffs had been turned, the spiritual leader of the community commanded attention by the ease and authority of his manner. His slender face was serene under a crown of graying hair, and his smile was warm. Having been in Wildrose long enough to be considered a part of it, Brother Victor had the respect of the people, probably their love.

The little woman at the organ was as devoted to the "work" as was her husband. In her, a plainness of attire was evident, enforced perhaps by her solemn responsibility to the biblical injunction to be "an example to the believers." But from underneath the brim of a hat devoid of ribbon or flower or feather, a stray lock of fair, fading hair wagged cheerful accompaniment to the vigorous peddling of her feet. And under a decorous blue serge skirt, her hips churned in unrestrained rhythm to the three/four time of the hymn. "Revival time," her soaring spirit sang, and Sister Victor's eyes closed and her chin lifted and her small, ringless hands pounded out the beat.

A ripple seemed to pass through the group as all eyes swung toward the door to observe the entrance of two elderly men, elbows held firmly by Willie Tucker and Sarah Thrum. The old men paused momentarily on unsteady feet, obviously enjoying the drama of the moment as whispers passed from mouth to mouth. Warm and welcoming hands reached out to them as they threaded their way toward a seat being vacated for them—in respect for the rarity of the occasion as much as for their age.

"Good ol' Willie!" people murmured, recognizing that patient man's faithfulness to the near-helpless brothers.

Others concluded that, since Sarah and her son came to look after them, Hubert and Harry Runyon seemed almost human again.

The boy, Simon, clung like a Saskatchewan leech to his great-great uncles and lodged himself proudly between them. He then opened a proffered hymn book to the proper selection. Elbow nudged elbow as the congregation watched Willie and Sarah find seats together. Muffled "I told you so" was repeated with "Well, I'll be!" as the congregation's attention turned again to Brother Victor.

Song leader as well as preacher, the pastor nodded an acknowledgment to the Runyon brothers, repeated the hymn number, and raised his hand for the downbeat: *"Blest be-e the tie-ee that binds . . ."* His strong tones lifted, the others joined in, and the opening hymn swelled through the open door and over the bush—a statement and a pledge—and latecomers were drawn to the circle of its promise.

The fervor of the singing was replaced by the fervor of the message, and Linn never noticed. The speaker's voice rose and fell, his finger pointed at appropriate times and his fist thumped to emphasize a point, and Linn neither heard the thump nor understood the point.

Restless feet, confined in Sunday shoes, shuffled on the oiled floor, and bodies shifted in seats never intended for adults, and Linn was unaware. Lost in a dream that had come true, Linn lived again the brief and breathless moments with Abram Weatherby, from the evening's unremarkable beginning to its surprising ending, and found the memory as sweet as the reality. After a night of sweet dreams, a slightly dazed breakfast, and morning chores, Linn now sat in the spot where, she felt, her life had changed in one brief half hour. And Abram—the reason for it all—sitting a few yards away! Linn felt she was the happiest girl in the world.

"Blest be the tie that binds," she sang, and felt it to be

a bond never known before, binding her irrevocably—and willingly—to Abram Weatherby.

Across the aisle, squeezed into a small desk beside the buxom girl who had said she would be among the pupils to gather for the opening of school in just one day's time, Kate Mason found her thoughts straying too.

Was it only yesterday she had turned from the train window where her quickened breath had left a small ring of fog, to fumble in her bag for the ticket marked for this remote area? Now yesterday seemed a million miles away and a hundred years ago.

At this moment a minister stood behind the battered desk that served as a pulpit; tomorrow *she* would stand there and begin her teaching career.

"O God!" Kate prayed, fervently and rather desperately and most earnestly, feeling she was caught in a trap of her own choosing. "Please help me!"

Kindly though they seemed, the faces that pressed around her were unfamiliar, many of them studying her covertly even as they turned in worn songbooks for the opening hymn. Above their heads four tall windows ranged down each side of the room; seated, she could see only the tips of the trees that pressed close to the fence that circled the schoolyard. It was all so strange . . . so different. Could she make the adjustment, from prairie to bush? Would these surroundings ever be home? Would these strangers ever be friends?

Of one thing she was certain: the smooth-faced, cold-eyed man with the improbable name of Gabriel Goss would never be part of her future.

The peal of the pump organ and the voices of the singers broke Kate's revery and called her to present circumstances. "We share our mutual woes, / Our mutual burdens bear," they sang, "And often for each other flows / The sympathizing tear."

It was a hymn Kate knew by heart. With a small shake

of her shoulders she dismissed yesterday and its strange new happenings and people, her distant family, the bush—both threatening and alluring—and lifted her voice, and her hopes, toward tomorrow's promise.

With the announcement of the benediction, hinges squealed and benches creaked as cramped bodies stood erect. With the amen, feet unaccustomed to midday inactivity shuffled on the oiled floor, and the congregation began a slow move toward the door.

Snatched from her daydreams, Linn Graham searched through the press of people for a glimpse of Abram Weatherby. Albin Trimble pushed past, offering plate in hand, heading for a private corner where he could count the scanty contributions—egg and cream money only, apparently; additional funds for the preacher's support would be forthcoming when the wagons of golden grain were trundled to town and sold and the faithful tithers brought in their tenth.

Torn between curiosity about the offering and her fretful concern for her daughters, Dolly Trimble hovered indecisively in front of Linn, her body rigid in its confining garments. "As rigid as her mind under her tight knot of hair," Judd was known to say, and to add, "The woman has to loosen her hairpins in order to blink!"

Those eyes, at the moment, were wide open and fixed balefully on Charity, who had allowed herself to be waylaid by Marc Szarvas. With his strong, square face—foreign!—sturdy body, and dogged determination, at 24 years of age Marc was ready to settle down. And it seemed his intentions were fixed on Charity Trimble. Linn, watching, concluded he just might be the one to handle the fractious girl.

Frustrated by Dolly's ironclad figure set foursquare in front of her, Linn sighed as Abram shouldered his way through the door. And when the new teacher looked at her and smiled, Linn turned her eyes with some reluctance from the receding back and introduced herself.

"I'm Linn," she said. "Linnet Graham. I live down the hill back of the school. The school grounds were originally part of my father's homestead."

"Well, then," smiled Kate Mason, "I'll probably see you often. I have an idea there may be times I'll need help, one way or another, and you'd be closest. This is my first teaching assignment, you know."

The conversation was interrupted as other members of the group, mothers particularly, crowded around to meet the teacher. This young woman would spend one school year, at least, in their midst. In her small hands they would place the care and education, perhaps the culture, of their offspring. Those hands, at first contact, appeared capable enough, and they turned away with relieved faces.

In spite of the eyes that were fixed on her critically and even anxiously, Kate Mason conducted herself with composure and dignity.

"She'll do," Linn decided, noting that the smile was warm and genuine, the brown hair and matching eyes ashine with health, the dress conservative.

But what, after all, did any of them know about style? A trip or two a year to Prince Albert, with limited funds to spend on personal items, and the few stores filled primarily with farm women who, like herself, were absorbed with obtaining the necessities of life. And for the least possible cost. To dress decently and, of course, warmly: that was the primary consideration.

With a surge of dissatisfaction, Linn smoothed her plain, dark skirt over her slim hips and determined that her next sewing project would be patterned more closely after the exciting magazine and newspaper fashions that were her chief contact with the outside world. And even they reached her late, often passing through many hands and numerous homes first. Perhaps a skirt made of red crepon cloth, lined throughout with percaline, interlined with crinoline, bound with velvet around the bottom, and with the new plait in back . . .

Dolly made a compulsive move toward her daughter, and Linn, brought back to reality, sidled past, leading the way through the desks to the entrance area with its lunch pail cupboard, scarred woodbox, and rough shelf holding a galvanized pail, with the communal dipper hanging beside it.

Outside, children were shrieking and chasing each other. Simon Thrum, Linn noticed, had deserted Hubert and Harry to play for a few brief moments with Corky and Cameron Rooney-Jameson. Simon's painful introduction to Wildrose had become a thing of the past, but Linn could remember the excitement involved when the district men banded together to rescue him from an attempted kidnapping. Out of that rescue had been born the blossoming love of his mother, Sarah, and bachelor Willie Tucker. Linn reflected sweetly on such a relationship and dared to reach within herself to explore such desires for her own life. Soon, no doubt, a wedding would be the outcome.

Husbands were bringing buggies and wagons around, and several young men were standing idly by the gate, obviously waiting, and obviously casually, for the girls who must pass through to the rigs beyond. Linn and Kate stopped willingly enough, and Linn made the introductions, going around the small circle until—face-to-face with him at last—"And this is Abram Weatherby."

Linn both needed to see Abram and dreaded doing so. So little had been said when he had taken her home, kissed her burning lips lightly, and left her in a turmoil of emotions that ran the gamut from dismay to disbelief to intoxication. She wondered if these were revealed in the face she lifted to him now.

But as the young people stood under the noon sun, bridging the gap from introduction to friendship with a few bright phrases, a few questions, a few explanations, and a few laughs, Abram's eyes were fixed on the fresh face of the young teacher.

It was Abram who stepped forward when Kate moved toward the Edwards' wagon. It was Abram who helped her gallantly—and uncharacteristically—into it, lingering over her hand. It was Abram who murmured, "I'll look forward to seeing you again . . ."

Abram turned from watching the rig drive over the brow of the hill and grinned at the other members of the group. His glance, passing over Linn indifferently, chilled her as abruptly as though he had hurled a handful of snow in her face. Her heart lurched, her expectancy flickered out, and a feeling of dismay replaced the anticipation that had trembled within her.

To talk casually with Abram seemed unreal—while the taste of those firm lips on hers lingered like sweet syrup. To see nothing special in his eyes seemed incredible—when she recalled so vividly how the ember in their dark depths had gleamed in the dim light through the schoolhouse windows. To imagine that his heart was beating normally, after her own had throbbed in rhythm with it and was even now moving strangely in her throat, caused her to feel as if she were in a dream. Or *was* last night a dream? she wondered somewhat wildly. A dream . . . or a nightmare!

"Abram!" she cried silently, as he bantered with the friends who had not misunderstood the small farewell scene. If his heart heard, his face failed to reflect it.

Finally, with a nod and a grin, Abram swung himself into the saddle and, with a jaunty smile, rode away. The gelding kicked up his heels in a gesture that seemed, somehow, to reflect the mood of the man who rode him.

With conversation swirling around her, Linn stood in a fog of unreality and uncertainty. And when the last buggy was gone and the final farewell spoken, she turned numbly homeward.

6

Celia Graham laid aside the poker and put the lid back on the cookstove, wiping a thin beading of moisture from her upper lip with the corner of her apron. The heat had raised a patina of color on her pale face, giving the lie, momentarily, to her frail health.

"How was the service?" she asked, turning toward the door as Linn stepped over the sill.

"Fine."

Celia's eyebrows raised at the noncommittal remark, and Linn, aware that her mother could read her well, added quickly, "The uncles were there."

"Hubert and Harry?" Unbelief tinged Celia's words. That Hubert and Harry, "uncles" to all and sundry, had darkened the door of the church at long last was news indeed.

"Yes," Linn continued, "and Simon—Simon-what's-his-name—"

"Thrum. Simon and Sarah, his mother. You know, Linnie, they came to Wildrose to take care of the uncles."

"I thought they'd never settle down this morning. Simon helped them get their specs on and found the hymn while Hubert and Harry wrangled, mostly without words, tugging on the hymn book."

"They would," Celia said softly. "How I wish I'd been there! Maybe next week. And the sermon, Linnie?"

"Oh, the sermon . . . it was about . . . ," Linn stumbled, and remembered that she had been lost in memories the entire hour. "It was about . . . God."

Catching sight of her mother's puzzled expression, she continued hastily, "And Samson and Delilah. You know—she cut his hair . . ."

"I'm aware of how and why Delilah cut Samson's hair," Celia said dryly. "As I remember, it was the theme of last Sunday's sermon."

"Oh, yes, and Dolly Trimble made the application that women shouldn't cut their hair, although why she would think that when it was Samson's hair that was cut . . ." Linn realized she was babbling and made an attempt to speak calmly. "You should have heard how she went on to-day."

"The sermon, Linn?" her mother pursued patiently.

"Oh, Mum," Linn managed, "my thoughts weren't on the sermon, I guess. Charity kept whispering to . . ." Linn paused, remembering. "She kept whispering to the new teacher."

"Of course—school starts tomorrow!" Celia, kept from the usual vital contact with her neighbors and the news of the community, was hungry for any scrap of information in her weary, dreary round of days and tasks.

"What's she like, Linnie?"

"Quite pretty, I suppose, if you like little brown wrens."

A look of surprise widened Celia's eyes, and Linn added quickly, "She's very nice, Mum. You'd like her."

And Linn escaped, to choose a dress at random and button herself into it with nerveless fingers. The green eyes looking back at her from the mirror over the chiffonier were their darkest—a mossy mix of yellows, browns, and greens, like dappled water, she had sometimes thought fancifully. Now they reflected hurt and humiliation, and a hint of anger.

Placing her hands on her flushed cheeks, Linn made an attempt to think rationally about Abram's unacceptable behavior that morning in light of his ardent embraces the night before.

"There's got to be some explanation," she forced herself to conclude, and waited until her breathing slowed and her eyes lightened.

Even so, she picked at the meal her mother had prepared. Finally she asked abruptly, "Do you mind if I clear up later?"

"I'll just throw a tea towel over things," her mother offered, "but," she continued, her eyes troubled, "is something wrong?"

Linn's voice sounded shrill even in her own ears. "Of course not! What could possibly be wrong? I'm just tired. The party last night . . . that stuffy schoolroom this morning . . ."

"Take a nap," Judd suggested practically. "*I'm* going to. I had a big night."

Judd's face was merry as he winked suggestively. But Linn knew the buggy had been in its usual place when she got home. Judd's big night, in comparison to her own, had undoubtedly been smoke where hers had been fire. Or had hers been smoke also?

Linn shivered and hoped passionately that her mother would never find out that she had been so foolish as to go into the dark schoolhouse with Abram. Even in the broad light of day it seemed a most unacceptable thing to do. "Courting trouble," her mother would have said, or worse.

The thought of her indiscretion and of Abram's careless response today was threatening to tarnish the experience, making it appear tawdry indeed, even in Linn's eyes. What would it look like to her mother? Linn shivered again.

Then, with a muttered exclamation, she leaped to her

feet and announced, "I'm thinking of going to town to work!" Her tone was strident and her words challenging.

Judd's mouth fell open. "What?" he squawked, while Celia's face whitened perceptibly.

"It isn't out of the question, is it?" Linn continued recklessly. "Marge went, and Leah, when school was out for them. I've been out two years! There's no future here—that's for sure!"

Judd set his cup down with a crash, and tea sloshed into the saucer.

"I could stay with Marge until I found a job," Linn rushed on. "If nothing else, I'll settle for being a hired girl somewhere!"

Celia's quiet voice broke the stunned silence that followed Linn's unexpected outburst. "Think about it, dear. If that's what you really want, we'll manage here somehow."

With her brother's, "Well, I'll be!" in her ears and aware of his shocked eyes on her back, Linn left the house for a hideaway she had frequented since childhood days.

As she stumbled toward the shady nook in the bush, she knew the pronouncement, spoken from a desperate heart and as surprising to her as it was to her mother and brother, was out of the question. Judd needed her, not only for the help she gave him and the work she did, but for encouragement. As for Mum—Linn's throat tightened—her weakening condition was frightening. There was no way Celia's frail shoulders could carry the massive burden of a homestead household.

"I'm caught," she thought helplessly.

Colorful foliage formed a leafy tunnel overhead and a shifting carpet of rusty reds and burnt yellows crunched underfoot, but Linn was oblivious to their beauty. Creeping into the familiar place, she crouched on a fallen log and dropped her head on her knees.

Eyes closed, she slipped again into Abram's embrace, and found it as sweet the second time around . . . sweet and meaningful. Until, that is, he turned an indifferent face to her, and his eyes, empty of memory, passed over her. Linn's slender body swayed with the pain of remembering.

To have given her heart so naively! To have believed it meant anything to Abram, and to have expressed herself so . . . warmly! "Darling" . . . had she actually whispered it?

Overcome by hurt and humiliation, Linn failed to hear the footsteps until a male voice spoke, with a note of surprise, "Hello!"

Linn's eyes lifted from dusty boots to well-shaped legs, narrow waist, broad shoulders, strong face, and darkly blue eyes, eyes in which the quick smile was turning to an expression of concern.

"I hope I didn't startle you," Trapper Farley said.

"No," Linn managed thickly, "you didn't."

Trapper Farley was not insensitive to women and their moods. But it didn't take a great deal of discernment to see the girl was in trouble. The casual remarks that had risen to his lips seemed inappropriate, and he said instead, "Look, can I help?" He was unprepared for the bitter twist of her lips and her rough response: "Go away! Just go away!"

But Trapp hesitated. Here was a girl he had noticed at the social because of the vivid expression of life in her multicolored eyes and the suggestion of laughter on her sweet lips, now hurting so badly it was painful to watch. Heaven knew he had no wish to get enmeshed in some girlish problem, but she was obviously troubled about something, even in anguish about it. Knowing she and her brother carried the burden of the homestead on their shoulders, his heart went out to her.

The young woman made an effort to speak reasonably, but her lips were rigid as she said, "Believe me—everything is all right. I wish you wouldn't trouble yourself."

But the white line about her mouth and the tense grip

of her hands said differently, and he pursued patiently, "Then may I get someone? Your mother, perhaps?"

"My mother!" Her wild laughter, prompted by some grim humor that escaped him, took him aback. "The last person in the world I want is my mother!"

And with that the girl jumped to her feet, placed her hand on his broad chest, gave him a violent push, and brushed past.

"Don't you know you're trespassing?" she flung at him from between gritted teeth.

Trapper Farley watched as the slim back disappeared around a bend in the lane and the bush hid the girl from view. "Now what do you suppose *that* was all about?" he said thoughtfully. And calling his dog, he followed the route the girl had taken.

The Cooley homestead—which he hoped in time would be thought of as the Farley place, for he intended to stay whether his cousin did or not—was back to back with the Graham homestead. Both touched on a small lake, and it was around this body of water Trapper Farley had been scouting when he ended up on Graham property and encountered the girl.

Her rude comment, flung at him as she fled past, was a fact: he was legally trespassing. But he doubted if anyone else had ever been accused of it. Fields and meadows were crossed at will; gates and doors were unlocked. Neighborliness was a way of life in the territories. Many strong and pressing needs, and not a few emergencies, bound people together.

There was in the young woman's cry a meaning beyond the fact that he was on property that didn't belong to him. He had invaded some personal domain, an area of privacy she protected to the point of fierceness: "Stay off! You're an interloper!"

When Trapp stepped into the clearing that was the

Graham farmyard, Judd was coming out of the log barn and waved a greeting.

"Hope I'm not trespassing," Trapp said as they met, with a brief thought for the girl's explosive accusation.

Judd snorted at the suggestion and took the proffered hand of his new neighbor.

"I understand it's the custom to reach our place through yours," Trapp said, "rather than going clear around the section by road."

"It's always been done," Judd agreed, and added with a certain wryness, "and it gives you quick access to most parts of the civilized world. Like Meridian."

Trapp Farley nodded, smiling. He already knew that beyond his place the virgin bush stretched almost unbroken to the banks of the Saskatchewan River.

"Sorry I haven't been over," Judd apologized. "How are you making out?"

"Pretty good, I guess," Trapp responded. "Except for the cabin. What a mess!"

"No one's lived there for a while."

"And it shows—mouse tracks, grain sacks, even a bird's nest or two! We, Boyd and I, aren't exactly used to living in the lap of luxury, but it would be nice to have the place clean, or at least cleaner than we've managed so far. Aside from a little chinking, some weatherstripping, and a good sweeping, we haven't done anything to it. Just moved in and unpacked."

Judd nodded sympathetically, agreeing that batching, at best, was no fun. And in that abandoned cabin . . .

"You don't have time to do things inside, that's for sure, not with all there is to do outside before snow flies."

"We have to locate a good team," Trapp agreed. "Our ponies are too light for farm work. We need a milk cow or two, a brood sow. Chickens and turkeys and so on will have to wait until spring, I suppose, and a garden—it's too late for that this year. We'll have to depend on the Meridian general store this winter. What we could do with right now," Trapp concluded thoughtfully, "is help to get that house in shape. Any ideas?"

"My sis could help," Judd said, adding almost immediately, "but she might be going to town."

"I wouldn't think of bothering her," Trapp said hastily.

"You might get Berry Lille."

"Berry Lille?"

"You haven't met the Lilles? Half Indian, you know. They live due north of you, just around the edge of the lake on the other side of your place. If you can call it a lake," the young man grimaced. "Boggy-bottomed, full of leeches. Just the same, we swam in it when we were young. And so did Berry."

"Still mighty young," the older man thought, studying the fresh young face, so open and friendly, yet shadowed with the responsibilities that were his since the death of his father. Aloud he said, "How do I get hold of this—Berry, is it?"

"Yeah, Berry. That's B-E-R-R-Y, like in *rasp*-berry. And you don't get hold of her." A grin split Judd's sunburned face until his teeth gleamed white. "Not that I've tried, you understand, but I know fellows who have. You shouldn't, unless you're a lion tamer."

Trapp didn't enlarge on his taming qualifications or the lack of them, and Judd continued, "Well, anyway, just follow the edge of the lake from your buildings to theirs, if you're walking, or take the section road on past your place if you're driving. You'll come across them easily enough. Nobody else much lives over that way as yet."

Trapper Farley thanked his young neighbor, shook hands, and turned toward the track that led to an open gate in the fence between the farms. If he had thought to look back, or cared to, he might have seen the curtain in the window of the Graham house drop into place.

7

FOLLOWING HER OUTBURST AT TRAPPER FARLEY
and in despair over Abram's incomprehensible behavior, Linn had gone to bed to brood until she slipped, at last,
into sleep and oblivion. It was with reluctance she forced
herself awake in the morning.

Downstairs, she found that Judd had preceded her
and had lit a fire in the range before going to the barn. Automatically, Linn pulled the teakettle to the front lid,
dipped water into a pot for oatmeal, reached for a loaf of
bread, and began dreading the day and her miserable
thoughts.

"I'll do that."

Celia, pale and swollen-eyed, took the bread from her
daughter's hand and began methodically cutting slices for
the wire toaster rack she had placed on the stove. "I'm
fine," she said reassuringly, and studied Linn's face. "And
you've got enough to do."

Celia went about the routine of fixing the morning
meal, and Linn, with an empty pail swinging in her hand,
stepped outside and turned toward the well, moving listlessly through couch grass so heavily diamonded with
dew that the yard, in the bright morning sun, shimmered
blindingly.

"Hey!" Judd hollered from the barn door. "If you'll
leave that, I'll do it!"

When his sister gave no indication that she heard, Judd shrugged, ducked his head, and went back to his cows.

The pail dropped from Linn's hand to tumble down the narrow shaft, splash, tip, and disappear. Hauled dripping to the surface and hoisted over the side of the well, the icy water splashed onto her slim bare legs but was scarcely colder than the heart beneath the faded calico.

As she turned to the house, Linn's gaze came to rest on the hill and the sun-touched schoolhouse, and she wondered if the district's newest arrival had any idea of the turmoil her coming had created. Still, Linn couldn't blame Kate Mason.

But Abram—with pain she relived the scene: she, Linn, turning enraptured eyes (she writhed to think of it!) toward him; he, Abram, ignoring her, turning seeking eyes on . . . someone else.

Novels and magazines played heavily and dramatically on the theme of the woman loved and tossed aside. Oh, that Abram would play so false a game! For game it was with him, she was beginning to suspect. But here in this isolated corner of the world, love was supposedly for keeps.

Linn gritted her teeth in a pattern that she was to follow throughout the day as she swung from despair to hope to dejection to resignation and back to optimism, picked up the pail, and headed for the house and Monday's routine.

Judd set up the washtubs before he went to his day's work in the fields and dipped the hot water into them. Linn pushed up her sleeves, grasped the handle of the galvanized stomper, and assaulted the first load of laundry mercilessly.

"Take it easy, Linnie," Celia cautioned, as she tossed another handful of soap shavings into the tub. "You'll never last the day at this rate."

Linn blew a strand of hair from her face and redoubled her efforts, finding a grim sort of comfort in the protest her body made, diverting her attention from the hurt in her heart.

But in the afternoon, gathering an armful of sun-sweet clothes from the line, the whoops of children released from school drew her eyes again to the hilltop. Her heart seemed momentarily to stop beating. A familiar buggy and mare were tied to the fence. Abram Weatherby—on the afternoon of a busy day in the middle of harvest—was inside . . . with someone else.

Stooping dazedly for the basket, Linn's eyes focused on a late-blooming rose at her feet, caught in a tangle of thistle. The weed clutched the sturdy bud in an embrace that seemed, in that moment, indecent. Somewhere inside of Linn an anger, not anticipated or understood, erupted, and disregarding both thistle and thorn and insensible to the wounds to her hands and the tender flesh of her wrists, she tore the offending sow thistle out by its roots and flung it into the bush with a gesture of loathing—and felt strangely relieved.

Celia, startled, watched the small drama from the kitchen window.

"Oh, that it were that simple!" she mourned, and let the curtain fall into place. "Lord," she cried helplessly in a time-worn plea, "help my girl! Don't let her be hurt!"

But unless the good Lord answered retroactively, it was a prayer wasted. Linnie was obviously already deeply hurt.

* * *

When the last child had clumped out the doorway, his lunch pail in his hand—a Golden Syrup pail, as they all were, with his name scratched on it—Kate collapsed at her desk.

"One day down! Two hundred—and how many to go?"

All in all, it hadn't been a bad day. Two dozen children of all ages and sizes had shown the innate politeness of these backwoods people. Folks across the territories took the matter of education seriously. The Wildrose school had been erected before some of the district's houses were completed, and the first structure, of log, had been replaced by a frame building while log houses were still going up. Meeting at first only during summer months because children were not equipped for the long, cold winter walk, school now kept a regular schedule. Rarely were children kept out of school to do farmwork.

Kate was cleaning the blackboard when she heard the sound of a horse and rig.

"Oh, no," she moaned.

Leaving home for school that morning, her arms loaded, Gabriel Goss had pulled the buggy up to the door and, with a cold smile, announced that John Edwards had decided Kate should have a ride to school this first day.

What choice did she have? But it was an awkward two miles, with Gabe's knee persistently pressing her own. Finally, in exasperation, Kate had dangled her lunch pail over her lap so that the man's next sly move in her direction was foiled by the presence of the tin pail.

Gabriel's face had flamed red under his tan, and his eyes had glittered alarmingly. In spite of that, Kate had said as she jumped from the buggy and gathered up her materials, "I want to walk after this, Mr. Goss. Don't come for me."

Now, her back pressed against the blackboard, Kate waited.

A black—not sleek blond—head appeared around the corner; a black head of hair above white teeth and a jaunty smile, and Kate quickly recollected the attentive young man she had met after church the day before.

"Well, hello! Mr. Weatherby, isn't it?"

"Abram." Abram bounded into the room and made his way rapidly toward the front. "I told you I'd be seeing you . . . and here I am . . . seeing you." His eyes told Kate that he very much liked what he saw.

"Abram—," Kate said coolly, "what can I do for you?"

"It's what *I* can do for *you!*" the brash young man responded. "Which is—give you a ride home."

Kate opened her mouth to explain that she preferred to walk.

"You have to be tired after your first day," Abram said coaxingly. "I'm going your way. You'll save shoe leather . . . and . . . and . . ." As though inspired, Abram concluded triumphantly, "I can tell you all about Wildrose—its flora and fauna. Now these," he indicated the jar of flowers on her desk, "are goldenrod."

"I know goldenrod," Kate said, smiling in spite of herself. "And I know roses."

"Ah, but do you know *asclepiad?*"

"Asclep . . ."

"Milkweed! See what I've taught you already? And there's so much more I can teach you."

Kate's back stiffened, but the merry face before her seemed so full of fun that she relented, allowed Abram to help her gather up her things, and headed home with more laughter than she had known in one short hour at any time in her life.

* * *

The early-morning air was tangy with the fragrance of bush and field when Trapper Farley opened the gate to the Lille farm, remounted, and rode leisurely up the narrow lane. The oncoming winter was yielding to the seduction of the late-summer sun.

"How many more days can we get like this?" Trapp wondered, reminding himself of the urgency of his mission here on the farm of the Lille family.

The dog's bark brought a man to the porch affixed to the log house. "Get down and come on in," he invited when Trapp approached. The voice, resonant and throaty, issued from a pockmarked, heavy face in which deep-set eyes squinted above broad cheekbones. The brown hand the man extended was cracked and calloused. "I'm Joe Lille."

Situated as close to Batoche as they were, Trapper wondered fleetingly if Joe Lille had been involved in the not-too-distant rebellion under Louis Riel when the métis—carrying the ancestry of both Indian and white and the inheritors of two lifestyles—found themselves at home with neither, challenged the new era, and lost. In the process many had forfeited the remaining pride they had, as well as their belongings, and had scattered to the north, to the Peace River country, and even to the United States. Others had quietly taken up the struggle to make a living along with the rising tide of immigrants. Surprisingly, they were accepted with little ill feeling.

The rebellion had not been without its good results. The growing importance of the Northwest Territories was being recognized. Now, nearing the turn of the century, their need for stronger government was clear. Soon, it was believed, the vast area between Manitoba and British Columbia would be divided into the self-governing provinces of Alberta and Saskatchewan.

"I'm Trapper Farley, your new neighbor," Trapp explained, following the hulking man into the small house. Here Ruby Lille, a comfortable, soft-fleshed woman, shook his hand and pointed him to a straight-backed chair at the side of a table. Turning to the range, she poured a cup of hot coffee and set it before her guest, pushing cream and sugar toward him.

"Thanks," Trapp said with a warm smile. "Boyd, my cousin, and I, are batching it . . . our coffee leaves a lot to be desired. I'm sorry to call so early in the morning," he continued and plunged into his reason for coming. "We find ourselves in sort of a bind . . . too much to do . . . too little time to do it. Judd Graham thought I might talk to you—"

At the faint sound of a footfall Trapper Farley turned, almost as though he had been expecting it.

"This is our daughter, Berry."

Who could blame the mother if her voice was tinged with pride? For the girl was lovely. She moved across the room with the fluid movements of some wild thing, a young deer, perhaps. Trapper Farley imagined momentarily that there would be the fragrance of all outdoors about her.

Shaking himself for being fanciful, he acknowledged the introduction with a nod and a smile and turned to Ruby and continued, "He—Judd—thought you might know of someone who could give us a hand with our house. We'd pay, of course."

Ruby Lille's eyes went to Berry's. The girl was gazing out of the window with unfathomable eyes. Silence reigned; somewhere a hen cackled. The dog on the porch thumped his tail.

Finally, Trapp cleared his throat. "Don't worry about us," he said. "We'll find someone."

"I'll come." Berry's voice was low and musical—songbirds . . . running water . . . rustling leaves. Trapper Farley checked his thoughts abruptly.

Without further ado, he made the necessary arrangements, refused a second cup of coffee, expressed his thanks, and rose to leave. Berry would follow immediately and come daily until the job was completed and the house clean and habitable.

Before the Lille buggy pulled into the yard, the Farley cousins had a hot fire roaring in the range and a battered copper boiler on its rusty top, filled with water. They also made a hasty attempt to straighten their personal belongings and swabbed their dirty dishes and turned them upside down on a towel to dry.

"Some washerwoman you are," growled Trapp. "Look at the color of that towel!"

"It's the same color as your Sunday shirt," his cousin

said reflectively. Trapp's rejoinder was cut off by the sound of the rig.

While his cousin went to meet the girl, Boyd Farley paused in the shadow of the porch. The young woman stepped down lithely and turned to the buggy seat for a box of cleaning materials. Her movements, Boyd thought, were as sinuous as those of the cat rubbing itself against his leg.

"Here," he said, stepping out of the shadows. "Let me have that."

The girl lifted eyes as sooty as the hair that fell in a silken cascade down her back.

"I'm Boyd Farley, Trapper's cousin." Boyd led the way into the cabin and was almost startled, upon turning, to find the girl at his shoulder. Her dark eyes met his; her gaze, he thought, was as straightforward and uninhibited as—the cat's.

"You are much alike," she said in her low voice, "you and your cousin."

"That's what everyone says. We're double cousins, so I suppose it's natural. We're some different though. For one thing," and the tall man grinned, "I'm not as well-behaved as Trapp."

"Me," the girl said quietly, "I am very well-behaved."

In a moment she was at work. Boyd, his jaw hanging open, found his face in an unaccustomed flush as he turned toward the door.

"Whew!" he said in an undertone as he and Trapp made their way to the barn. "I don't think she knows whether or not I was serious. Now," he said with another grin, "I'll have to try to live up to my own reputation."

They agreed it was disconcerting to find such poise in anyone so young—the girl appeared to be about 16 or 17 years of age—and that there was in Berry a curious sense of being too old for her years, and too wise.

"She makes you think of a pool," Trapp offered reflec-

tively, "a very still pool." He added thoughtfully, "I wonder if it could be riffled."

"No man could be blamed for trying," Boyd answered
feelingly. "But," he added with a dramatic sigh, "pool rif-
fling isn't on the schedule, at least for today."

The cousins regretfully turned to the fence repairing
that awaited them.

When Trapper and Boyd came in at noon, Berry had
opened a can of beans, sliced the cheese she had located in
the skimpily supplied cupboard, and set out a loaf of
bread. As the men ate, she went outside and washed windows at the other end of the cabin.

At the afternoon's end the men came in to find the
windows clean inside and out, the heavy coat of dust
swept from the rough log walls, and the cupboards
scrubbed until their boards gleamed golden as the damp-
ness faded. The stove had been fired, the teakettle filled,
and the word "oilcloth" added to their list of supplies.
Berry was gone. And they were dismayed, but not surprised, to find she had fixed no supper.

"I wish I'd teamed up with a cook," Boyd said sourly
as he measured coffee grounds into the enamel pot, molli-
fied somewhat to find it emptied of its accumulation of
soggy grounds, and scrubbed.

"I cook as well as you wash clothes!" Trapp defended.

"Well, you know how to make bannock," Boyd reminded, "and you'd better get at it. The last crusts of this
store bread are hopeless. Moldy—even the mice don't
want it. I suppose it's beans for supper again."

And Boyd began opening cans. "One of us ought to
get married—and I vote for you."

When there was no response from his cousin, Boyd
glanced at Trapper in surprise. "Why," he grinned, "I believe you already thought of that!"

Trapp was chunking wood into the range, and his
cousin's comment went unacknowledged.

"Have you?" Boyd pursued. "Thought about marriage?"

"Not particularly," Trapper said.

"In general, perhaps?"

"What I have been feeling, as I pray about it," Trapp said thoughtfully, slipping the pan of bannock into the oven, "is that I really think Wildrose is the right place—for me, at least—to settle down."

Boyd grunted. He knew his cousin's commitment to knowing God's will for his life and the importance of prayer in finding it. Each had been raised by godly parents. Trapp, in particular, maintained a steadfast confidence that the Christian walk was the only way for him. Boyd, less vocal and perhaps less committed, nevertheless respected his cousin's stand. It had not been easy, he knew; the rough, vagabond sort of life they had shared as young men had served to settle and clarify Trapp's convictions, and, in a quiet way, he had deepened into what Boyd supposed was a "man of God."

"If so," Boyd followed up on his cousin's surprising announcement that he would settle permanently in Wildrose, "this is where you'll find the girl you'll marry—have you met any likely prospects?"

But Trapp was checking the bannock, and once again Boyd's question went unanswered.

The meal, somehow lonelier than usual, was quickly finished, and the men washed and dried the dishes with sighs of resignation, aware that, if they left them, Berry would think they expected her to do them. Though they had known her such a brief time, neither was sure she would.

But they settled down to sleep with a more contented feeling than they had known since arriving in Wildrose. Neither was ever to mention it if his dreams were filled with visions of a fleet-footed, lithe, and lissome figure, with flowing dark hair and enigmatic eyes, who slipped through the bush, forever just beyond reaching fingers.

8

A NOTHER NIGHT OF RESTLESS SLEEP. ANOTHER dreary dawn, in spite of a sun that seemed reluctant to trim its golden wick or dim its flame in the face of autumn's advance.

With her waking thought, Linn was back on an emotional merry-go-round, condemning herself and excusing Abram, defending herself and accusing him. It was becoming heart-wrenchingly clear, in her lucid moments, that what had been special and beautiful was threatened with sordidness unless she was able to get things into perspective.

With a clatter, Linn put the sadirons on the stove, determined to submerge thought with physical effort. While the sadirons heated she started the task of baking bread—a task so familiar she could do it automatically—measure, sift, stir, pummel. And this she did so savagely that Judd, dumping an armload of wood into the box beside the range, exclaimed, "No need to kill it, Sis!"

With the covered bread rising on the warm lid of the reservoir, Linn turned to the usually despised ironing, thumping the heavy irons down and heaving the bunglesome garments around until some of the soreness in her heart seemed to ease. If her accompanying "Stupid! Stupid! Stupid!" carried to Celia in her rocking chair, the mother never mentioned it. If Linn had been less caught up in her own woes, she might have caught Celia's pale lips in what looked suspiciously like whispered prayer.

When the ironing was finished and the bread, golden and crusty, was removed from the oven, Linn said, "I'm going out, Mum."

"I've been thinking," her mother called, and Linn slipped to the doorway between the two rooms. "We haven't been very neighborly to the Farley men. I should have invited them over for supper before this." Celia's tone was regretful, but it brightened as she added, "And I will—just as soon as I feel better. That bread, Linnie—it smells so good. Those men don't have anyone to bake for them. They might like a loaf. What do you think?"

Linn was agreeable. Besides, she knew she owed Trapper Farley an apology for her behavior when he had stumbled on her in the bush, too filled with her silly troubles to greet him sensibly or respond decently to his offer of help. If she was to face him in the future without embarrassment, it was important to clear the air.

"I'll take a loaf to them, Mum," she responded. "The walk through their woods is one of my favorites."

"Poor men," her mother said casually.

"Poor men?"

"That terrible cabin. Judd says it's hardly fit to live in. They're desperate—need badly to get it fixed up before snow flies and they're holed up in it for the winter."

"I see what you're getting at, Mum," Linn said, and kissed the top of her mother's gray head. "I'll offer to help. It won't hurt me—and it will make you feel better."

Her mother smiled her approval. But her face darkened as she said, "You've got more to do now than you can handle. I never intended that you should have to shoulder so much so early in life. I'm no help—" Celia's voice broke.

"Tommyrot!" Linn said strongly, and her mother smiled weakly, the reaction Linn had been hoping for.

"Why, you're getting stronger—I can tell!" Linn added stoutly.

But it wasn't so. The face Celia lifted to Linn now was

a mix of laughter and tears at her daughter's nonsense, but it was pale and peaked. And that in spite of faithful doses of Dr. Blane's Nerve and Brain Tablets, medicine they could little afford to have, and couldn't afford to be without.

But Linn, turning to the cupboard in search of a hoarded paper bag, was relieved to see her mother's cheerfulness restored.

Along with the warm bread, wrapped loosely to keep it from getting clammy, Linn added a bowl of fresh butter and, feeling expansive, a jar of brilliant pin cherry jelly, the best, in her mind, the bush had to offer. It was enough, she thought, to make amends for her churlish behavior when Trapper Farley had come face-to-face with her in the bush.

She changed into a fresh dress, ran a comb through her hair; the summer sun, she noted, hadn't helped its natural unusual mixture of colors. Then, "Look for me when you see me," she called to her mother. "Perhaps I'll stay the rest of the afternoon and help. Just so long as it isn't ironing!"

She crossed the yard to the gate and the track to the Farley place. Her heart, as well as her steps, was considerably lighter than it had been.

Bird song, so much a part of her life, often went unnoticed, but today she listened. "Only flying creatures sing," she mused with unaccustomed philosophy, "—those with wings." She hummed a tentative bar or two and laughed at her own foolishness.

The sun slanted through thinning foliage, and drying leaves drifted down, laying a multicolored carpet underfoot. Winter, the long season, would soon be upon them. But without fail—since time began in unbroken cycles—spring returned. In its time, earth responded to vagrant breezes, coaxing chinooks, and warming sun; birds returned from goodness knew where; flowers lifted bright faces from every nook and cranny; and green sprouts pushed through thawing soil. You could count on it. There was life after death—in the bush.

Linn breathed deeply and lifted her face to the sunshine and felt the hot, foolish, healing tears sting her eyes. Tears and song, for a few seconds, mingled as surely as the bitter and the sweet aspects of the bush joined to make life a joy and a despair.

It was here, in this quiet place and at this needful time, that prayer should have welled spontaneously, a healing balm. But Linn turned her thoughts quickly to more familiar ground—her own way for her own life. Knowing what she wanted, and uneasily aware that her will might not be God's, threatened the tenuous thread of peace offered now by the beauty of her surroundings. And in a moment the troubling inner voice was, once again, stilled.

Smoke was spilling lazily from the stovepipe of the Cooley—Farley—house. A dog raised his head and thumped his tail in a tentatively friendly manner as Linn approached the porch. Her fingers touched the top of his lifted head as she stepped past him to the door, her knock rattled the frame of the ancient screen.

There was a small sound from the interior, for the door was open, and suddenly Linn felt exposed, outlined in the bright light of the doorway, and awkward about visiting men alone.

About to put the sack down and turn on her heel and escape, the rickety screen opened and Trapper Farley's by-now familiar voice spoke—and, as in the bush meeting, with some surprise: "Hello again!"

It was not a good beginning; the man was, obviously, reminding her of their previous encounter—an encounter she would just as soon forget.

In the pocket of silence, Linn was aware that Trapper Farley, from the higher level of the kitchen floor, towered above her. She felt somehow disadvantaged; her awkwardness increased. When he opened the door and asked, "Will you come in?" she stepped up automatically to find, annoyingly, that he still towered above her.

With a burst of what seemed, at the time, to be sheer brilliance, and with an antagonism she didn't understand completely, she said sweetly, "I hope I didn't startle you," and felt the score was even.

Trapper Farley obviously recognized her use of his phrase; she was gratified to see the gleam that surfaced, briefly, in his eyes. Another small moment of silence followed, and in it Linn could almost hear the clashing of swords.

Linn wondered, belatedly, if it was forever too late to rectify the situation. It was.

"What have we here?" Trapper Farley was saying in a voice that was too smooth. He reached for the sack even as her nose picked up and recorded the combined odors of lye soap, brewing coffee, and, unmistakably, fresh-baked bread.

Instinctively, Linn's fingers tightened on the lumpy sack she held. To no avail. The fingers of a hand stronger than her own seemed to pry her grasp loose, while with his other hand Trapp drew the sack to him.

As Trapper Farley peered into the sack, Linn's eyes were riveted on a table topped with golden, crusty, cooling bread.

"Ah . . . ," Trapp breathed, "bread!"

"My mother . . . ," Linn spluttered, "it was my mother who thought—that is, we didn't know you baked."

Catching a definite glint of laughter in his eyes, she added defensively, "It was my mother's idea . . . she thought I ought to come over and, well—help out."

As the lame explanation stumbled from her lips, Linn noted the wildflowers in the jar on the table and the gleam of wax on the ancient wood, and it didn't take the slight sound from the corner of the room for the terrible truth to dawn on her: Trapper Farley wasn't alone.

Turning abruptly, Linn saw the slender form of Berry Lille at the side of the range, a pinafore cinched snugly about her small waist and a flower in her black hair.

"Berry! I didn't know you were here! That is . . . I thought Trapp was alone."

Trapper Farley's eyebrows rose, and Linn's face flamed.

"I mean . . ."

Trapp smiled sweetly and pulled out a kitchen chair. "Could I offer you something? Coffee, perhaps? Or better yet—cocoa?"

Fury built inside Linn at this reference to the social and her slopped drink. *I'll get him!* she seethed silently. *Believe me—if it's a fight he wants, it's a fight he'll get!* But it wasn't the right moment, with Berry listening and watching, a startled expression on her face.

Obviously Berry had performed minor miracles. The old stove gleamed, the towel above the washstand was spotless, the wooden cupboard had been oiled until it shone, dishes were orderly on the shelves, and pots and pans hung handily on nails on the log wall.

But she could have said something! Having gone through school with the half-Indian girl, Linn understood and accepted Berry's stoicism, but now it annoyed her.

When Trapp, watching Linn, explained, "Berry's been helping out," Linn murmured, "How nice"—and immediately wished she hadn't. Berry, after all, was perfectly innocent in all of this. Or was she?

It was blindingly clear, suddenly. No wonder she had felt like an interloper as she stood on the porch. The silence inside now took on meaning.

With that conclusion, Linn got to her feet.

"What? Going so soon?" the man asked. "By the way, have you recovered from your—er—problem?"

Linn stiffened. "You're mistaken," she said evenly. "There was no problem. It was the heat."

And although her lips managed a civil, "You're welcome," to Trapper Farley's, "Thanks so much for the bread . . . and jelly . . . and butter," as he was removing the items from the sack, her eyes, she felt sure, were shooting green sparks at the amused face of the man who held the door open for her when she took her departure.

Only later, when anger simmered down, did Linn realize she had never offered an apology for her rude performance at their last meeting.

And now it seemed she had added insult to injury.

S ANDWICHED BETWEEN A TOO-SHORT SUMMER and an overlong winter, the autumn party would be a night to remember. And these were few enough for the people of the Canadian bush. Soon their world would be mantled with snow, and all their efforts would go into simple survival: chopping wood, shoveling snow, breaking ice in troughs and water pails, stuffing fodder of one kind or another into the hungry maws of patient, cud-chewing cows, impatient, stamping horses, steadily-blazing kitchen ranges, iron-bellied heaters, and families with little else to look forward to in an endless succession of gray days in cramped quarters.

From miles around they would come, child and adult alike, eager for a break in the routine. Wives prepared special dishes, packing boxes to overflowing; children anticipated treats not enjoyed on any other occasion. Young girls preened before mirrors and fixed their hair in unaccustomed styles, filed and buffed nails broken by the day's work and play, dabbed toilet water behind their ears, and dreamed certain dreams. Dreams were free in Wildrose.

Half-grown boys made plans to push over the school toilets, not realizing the prank was as old as the two-seaters themselves, with only the pranksters changing year by year.

Young men, more adept with stubbled fields than

stubbled faces, ran roughened hands over downy chins, shaved whether they needed to or not, and hoped the soap's fragrance would linger in lieu of the lotion that few, if any, had. A few fortunate ones slipped hoarded mints into their pockets and laid plans for persuasive encounters with certain young females.

In the Trimble household Dolly had much to concern her, more than the usual banking of the fires, checking Albin's shoes for barnyard scrapings, and making sure her daughters were decently turned out.

"Here he is!" young Harmony squealed, and Modesty caught her breath and put a hand to her hair, checking the pins that held it in its unaccustomed top knot.

Modesty, with no modesty at all, was hurrying on light feet toward the door when Dolly intercepted her oldest daughter with a harsh, "Hold on, Miss!" Modesty paused, turning aside reluctantly to the corner of the room where her mother stood, beckoning her imperiously. It was always serious when her mother said "Miss."

"I'm counting on you, Missy, to remember to conduct yourself at all times with—restraint!"

"Yes, Mum," Modesty promised promptly. Too promptly, Dolly thought, and her face became grim when Modesty's eyes went past her mother to the door, where Charity was welcoming Judd.

Now, noting the spark in her second daughter's eyes, Dolly's concern shifted.

"Charity!"

Charity started. "What? What?" she asked.

When her mother motioned her back from the young couple, a stubborn look settled on Charity's round and pretty face. "Oh, Ma," she muttered, while Dolly hustled to the door, severity in every line of her face.

"Judd," she said with terrible firmness, "I expect you to bring Modesty straight home."

"Of course, Mrs. Trimble." Judd made his promise as

promptly as Modesty had made hers, and Dolly was no more satisfied with his than with hers.

Judd, like everyone else, was well aware of Dolly's anxieties where her daughters were concerned and, if he valued his budding relationship with Modesty, he would be careful, very careful indeed.

But schoolhouse and home were two miles apart, and horses could walk mighty slow. Very serious courting could be done in a buggy, and Judd's eyes shone in anticipation of it.

From Dolly in her black dress, hovering over them like a wounded crow, the young couple made their escape.

"It's not fair!" Charity wailed as soon as the door had closed.

"Now, Miss," warned her mother, "don't start that again."

"I'm old enough," Charity said tightly. "And Marc . . . Marc Szarvas . . ."

"Never," Dolly's tones were emphatic. "Never the son of that immigrant family."

Charity's mouth opened to protest, but before she could speak, Dolly warned sharply, "When you're *mature* enough you may have a well-chaperoned date. But never, *never* with Marc Szarvas.

"Now get your coat. Your father and little sister are waiting in the wagon. See if you can't manage to have a good time—without the boys."

Blowing out the lamp, Dolly failed to see the mutinous look on the face of her middle daughter.

* * *

John Edwards tucked a blanket around his wife's feet and climbed into the buggy beside her. "Gabe and Kate are both gone already, I notice," he said. "I don't suppose they went together."

"Silly!" scoffed Maggie. "Although I wouldn't put it past him to have asked her. You know, John, he is being a little obnoxious—if one can be a little obnoxious. Actually, he's being a real . . . pill, and that's the kindest word I can use."

John threw back his head and laughed heartily. The horse picked up his ears and quickened his step.

"I'm betting Kate can look after herself," John said. "But how did she go? I heard a rig drive away an hour or so ago."

Maggie's answer was thoughtful. "It was Abram Weatherby, of course."

"So it's true," John said, as the buggy turned from their lane to the section road. "They really *are* interested in each other. Seems fast."

"Yes, very fast. But Kate's a mature young lady, John. That's been obvious from the start. And Abram has his farm and his house, and," Maggie's voice was thoughtful again, "I suppose he thinks he needs a wife."

"She doesn't seem like his type, though."

"Opposites attract, they say. His type—fun-loving, always fooling around—often settle down with someone more serious. He's played the field long enough; it's time he made up his mind, though it may break the hearts of a lot of girls, not to mention their mothers."

"Well, Kate was raised on a farm."

"She'll make a good farmer's wife. Anyone can learn, if they want to, raised on a farm or not."

John's response was low. "You should know."

"I know."

Eventually, "And—has it been worth it, Maggie?" John's voice had dropped even lower until it was almost lost in the creaking of the harness and the rattling of the rig.

"Never doubt it, John."

"No regrets?"

"No regrets."

"Nor for me. Sometimes, though, I can't believe we go off to something as unsophisticated as this party."

"And enjoy it. Don't worry about me, John. I love our life. I love Wildrose."

John slipped his hand out of his glove, took Maggie's hand in his, and in a silence that throbbed with meaning to them both, they smiled at each other and bounced over the frozen, rutted road to a gathering of good friends, deep in the remoteness of the Canadian bush.

* * *

Linn Graham prepared herself for the evening with mixed emotions—an eagerness to see Abram, and a nagging dread to do so. The days and weeks had passed with no word or even a meaningful look from him, and she was finding it difficult indeed to rationalize the situation.

But hope wouldn't die, or young love. "He's decided to take things a little slower," she comforted herself at first. Or, recalling Abram's ardor, "It's my fault. I said wait. My reaction has been a puzzle to him."

But remembering her spontaneous "darling," Linn buried her face in her hands and could have wept for her innocent outburst to what may have been meaningless to Abram after all.

One thing was crystal clear: she would have to let him know her true feelings, without pretense, or coyness, or false modesty. And tonight was the time to do it.

What had flamed once, however briefly, could be lit again.

Lamp in hand, Linn leaned toward the mirror and watched her lips curve in what she hoped was an inviting smile and her eyes soften meaningfully, planning an encounter that would remove the barrier between her and Abram Weatherby.

But the golden shafts of light in the mossy eyes reflected a touch of desperation mingled with anticipation. And she made the short walk up the hill to the schoolhouse with a mix of expectation and dread as she contemplated the bold move she must make.

When Linn entered the hurly-burly of the room and saw Abram's face, her heart leaped, for it was turned toward her with an open invitation in his laughing eyes. "The darling . . . ," she whispered and her pulse raced. Impulsively she took a step toward him.

"Hey, Marc! Marc Szarvas!" Abram called over her head. "C'mon over here!"

Marc Szarvas crowded past. Blindly, Linn turned aside, the eagerness in her eyes doused by the tears that filled them. Dropping her head to hide the telltale sign of her humiliation and hurt, she thrust herself through the crowd and headed toward the door, and escape.

"Excuse me . . . ," she murmured thickly, and found her hands gripped as they pushed at the male chest blocking her passage.

"Is it just me," asked an amused voice, "or do you treat all men this way?"

Linn looked up, inches away from eyes with a touch of laughter in their dark depths.

But Trapper Farley's face sobered immediately as if, in that moment, he had seen into her heart and discovered the reason for the shimmer of tears and the pain-twisted mouth.

Held against him momentarily by the unexpectedness of the encounter and the press of the noisy crowd—too many people for so small a space—Linn watched as Trapper Farley's gaze lifted and moved across the room to Abram Weatherby who, face flushed, was engaged with Kate Mason in some childish activity to which no man in his normal frame of mind would give a moment of his time. And when that gaze moved back to her face, Linn thought she saw a budding comprehension in it, wrenched her hands free, and fled toward the door—but not too rapidly or blindly to see the lovely, impassive face of Berry Lille at Trapp's shoulder.

"I believe I hate that man!" she gritted as she stumbled down the steps. But whether it was Trapper Farley or Abram Weatherby she meant was not clear.

Linn leaned her arms on the fence railing and laid her hot face against them. Why was this stranger the one to glimpse what was troubling her? For it seemed that Trapper Farley had seen and correctly interpreted the little byplay.

The frigid air, now laced liberally with chilling rain, had its effect on her overheated body; Linn shook with the cold and the emotions that racked her. She longed to escape, but her coat was inside. Besides, to go home was to face her mother's questions. She felt wretchedly caught in the unhappy situation.

She had decided to go back and face the evening's dreary misery with as bold a front as she could muster when the door opened and a female figure slipped out, outlined momentarily against the light from the door. But in that brief glance, Linn recognized the buxom, bouncing shape.

Charity disappeared quickly around the corner of the building; as Linn stepped again toward the door, it opened again, revealing the slim figure of a man. As he paused on the step and lit a cigarette, the matchlight highlighted the face of Gabriel Goss.

Linn was unbearably cold but waited, reluctant to face Gabriel's raised eyebrows and suggestive smirk. But he, too, quickly slipped around the corner and disappeared. Linn, wondering briefly if the small "necessary" buildings were still in upright position, made a dash for the door.

Inside, amid the fun and frolic and under the thoughtful gaze of Trapper Farley and no gaze at all from Abram Weatherby, Linn, head high, heart heavy, smiled the night away.

10

STORM WINDOWS WERE IN PLACE, WOODPILES bulged in every yard, dirt mixed with straw had been packed around foundations of houses and barns and chicken houses. Cellars were stocked with home-grown and home-canned food, and a supply of staples filled each cupboard against the time when it would be difficult, even impossible, to make a trip to Meridian.

Wagon beds were lifted from wheels and put in place on sleigh runners in anticipation of the time when the clouds would open and the great snows come. Buggies jolted over rut-frozen roads, and animals grew shaggy coats and huddled with their backs hunched into the north winds. Trees were stripped bare of leaves and occasionally, as their life-flow froze, they snapped with small explosive sounds. The thermometer dropped; and still the snow held off.

Kate enjoyed the walk to school each morning, acquainting herself with Wildrose. It was so different from the unending plateaus of grass and grain to the south, where the long skyline was broken, and that rarely, by the jutting outlines of house and barn and granary. Here houses, usually small and routinely whitewashed, huddled in the bush. Frame houses—built when some folks had arrived with enough ready cash—were uniformly unpainted, weathered a silvery gray that blended graciously with their surroundings.

Nowhere did one see the remains of soddies such as had dotted the western plains by the thousands not too many years before. Kate's mother had been born in one. Her grandmother, a woman of some culture, had followed a man hungry for the land that was the cheapest and some of the best in the world. The walls of their first home had been squares of sod cut from the hard prairie grassland; its roof, poplar poles covered with layers of hay, pieces of sod and dirt—government shingles, they were called.

Although wonderfully warm in winter and cool in summer, life in a soddy had been unbearably crude. But farms had slowly evolved; great stretches of grain greened and then golded the prairies. By comparison, farms here in the bush were small, the growing season short and uncertain; they would never know the dust storms and sweeping blizzards of the open land, however.

"Here," Kate thought, "there was a combination of the bitter and the sweet, the harshness of the rough thistle and the haunting fragrance of the sturdy, five-petaled wild rose."

Although she walked in the morning, when school was done for the day and she had said good-bye to the last child, more times than not the door would open and Abram Weatherby would enter, a smile crinkling his blue eyes and brown cheeks. As she would close the damper, straighten her desk, and gather up her things, he would watch lazily from a back bench. Then he would put her in his buggy, tuck a cover around her, and rattle over rough roads until she thought she couldn't go another mile. Then he would pull her close and laugh into her eyes.

"He's good for me," she thought. "I'm inclined to be serious, and he's always full of fun."

* * *

All the shallow sloughs and puddles of water froze. The "rubber" ice on the lakes—such fun to walk on and so dangerous—became rock solid. And still it hadn't snowed.

Now was the ideal time for a skating party; later the ice would be deep in snow and skating confined to a small rink after it had been laboriously scraped.

Among several lakes, Graham Lake was the most centrally located. And there was a small log building at the lake's edge, commonly and facetiously called the clubhouse, which served to warm skaters who must stop from time to time to loosen skates and rub numb feet; chilblains were always a threat.

"If you'll check the clubhouse," Judd told his sister the day of the event, "I'll rustle down some wood." It was the usual procedure, and Linn took off for the lake willingly with a shovel for emptying old ashes and a broom for sweeping the benches.

She had not failed to note Abram's buggy at the schoolhouse many days, and she was often morose and depressed. Not having carried out her plan to talk to him, she eventually found herself avoiding him. Once, cutting off his casual greeting, she caught a quizzical glance from his eyes and had felt her face flush before she turned away.

"He *does* remember," she thought, and didn't know whether she felt better or worse for the knowledge.

An evening of skating would be a welcome diversion. Winter, the long dark season, had barely begun, and already Linn was finding its enforced hibernation oppressive.

In spite of fears that it would snow after all and spoil the plans, the evening was clear. Buggies piled up in the Graham yard and along the schoolhouse fence, and laughing people, young and old alike, made their way to the lake.

Trapper and Boyd Farley hiked over the frozen lake from their place, stopping for Berry Lille along the way. Berry was darkly beautiful in a scarlet hood, while the light from the lantern hung at the clubhouse door glowed like a sapphire on Linn's blue tam and scarf; Kate's white toque sat on her brown head like a casual crown.

A moon shone overhead in a cloudless sky and followed underfoot as the group skated, a brilliant reflection in the glasslike lake. Skate blades sliced carelessly through a million stars, while hair, tossed with the speed of the skater's flight, tangled, it seemed, with a million more.

Abram monopolized Kate from the beginning. The same crisp air that brought color to her cheeks brought the blood coursing warmly through the veins of the young man.

Kate had not discouraged Abram's attentions, but there was about her a quiet reserve that tantalized him, made him uncertain of her interest. And Abram wasn't used to that.

Suddenly he had to know. He had played around long enough. Coming to an abrupt halt in the middle of the lake and swinging himself around in front of her, Abram tipped Kate's face up with a gloved finger. She looked back steadily. There was something in that level gaze, that dignified demeanor, those mature ways, that challenged his lightheartedness.

There in the moonlight he put his arms around her and pulled her close, as close as bulky wraps would allow, her face still raised to his as if she knew the serious moment—rare with this gregarious man—had come.

Huskily Abram said, "Katy, marry me," and continued searching those steady eyes, wanting to make them change.

But it was not until he added "I love you" that warmth flooded her eyes—and gave him his answer.

In the clubhouse, Charity allowed Marc to tie her skates, relishing the sight of the strong man kneeling before her. Catching her pleased expression, Marc sat back on his heels and said, in the usual light manner he consistently used with her, "All right, Miss Smarty, you can go."

"Come skate with me," Charity teased through lowered lashes. "Maybe I've forgotten how . . . maybe I'll fall!"

Marc knew she was flirting. Holding her arm, he guided her through the circling legs and feet of those seated on the benches in the clubhouse around the blazing heater—out onto the ice.

For a while they skated in silence, caught up in the pleasure of the first skate of the year. The circle was to the right, and the entire lake was dotted with skaters, alone or in couples, with bands of children hand in hand.

"Have you got your ski legs yet?" Marc asked jokingly, and Charity laughed.

But as he loosed his hands from their crossed-arm grip, Charity complained, "My skate's loose!"

At her insistence they turned to the lake edge and seated themselves on a fallen log. Charity extended her foot. Marc knelt, tested the laces, then raised his eyes to hers and said, in slightly mocking tones, "All right—out with it. What's really on your mind? Or is it just that you like seeing me on my knees?"

"You never take me seriously!" Charity pouted, thoroughly enjoying the moment.

Marc studied her face a moment, then seated himself at her side, wondering how to handle this. His natural instincts were to take her in his arms, but he had set himself a rigid regimen, and he knew it could be quickly shattered, and probably with consequences, if he weakened. Charity's age, her mother's objections, his plan to establish his own homestead—it would all fall into place, but it would take time.

"Charity, my sweet . . ." Marc paused, uncertain how much to reveal.

With glowing eyes in the moonlight, Charity turned her face up to his. For an agonizing moment Marc hesitated. She seemed so much older than she was, so ready for love. Because he loved her, Marc knew he must proceed with caution. An awakened Charity would be hard to control.

With a groan, Marc took Charity's chin between the finger and thumb of his gloved hand and turned her face from him.

"Behave yourself, you scamp," he said thickly.

The glow in Charity's eyes faded, and the expectancy. Even in the moonlight Marc could see the sulkiness of her mouth. That she was both hurt and angry he knew, and he said more gently and quite seriously, "Listen to me. If you're so grown up, try to understand. I'm only going to say this once, Cherry: I want to kiss you . . . I want to! But it's too soon . . . it's too soon. Don't you see? You're too young. And this isn't play—not for me."

With an angry cry, Charity thrust herself off the log and onto the lake. "Too young! I'm sick of hearing I'm too young!"

With considerable inner pain and some exasperation, Marc watched Charity's flying figure zigzagging toward the cabin.

"Old enough to want to be a woman" was his thought, "but too childish to handle it. Just wait, my love, just wait."

And he dared to hope she would.

As always when Abram was present, Linn was overcome with conflicting emotions. Seeing him tonight with Kate Mason, her hopes of a happy evening went out on a sigh and a groan. Escaping the young men clamoring for a skate, she made her way to the far end of the lake. There, away from curious eyes, she skated in tight circles, blind to the night's beauty.

"If only . . . if only . . ." She couldn't finish the sentence. And prayer eluded her; somehow she couldn't bring herself to plead for the love of Abram Weatherby. And a prayer of submission to God's will—it wasn't easy to give up dreams! And so the comfort Linn might have known eluded her.

Someday, some future day, such submission would be reasonable. Now, with the confidence of the young and headstrong, Linn was sure—though somewhat uneasily sure—that she knew what was best.

"People have died of broken hearts," she thought now, darkly, clutching her misery to her. "It'll be my luck to live." With this cheerless thought, her good humor reasserted itself, the twisted lines of her mouth relaxed, and she was able to move back toward the clubhouse and join the others as they crowded inside for refreshments.

But her cup of cocoa jerked and spilled onto her hand, and she never felt the burn when an exuberant Abram pulled Kate through the door and announced, "Surprise! Katy and I are getting married!"

Amid the spontaneous outburst of well-wishes, Linn congratulated herself on her self-control and success in remaining impassive. Why then did she flash a glance at the only other person who might see through the charade and suspect her true feelings? Trapper Farley's dark eyes met hers over the heads of the boisterous people.

Linn's chin lifted, and she looked at him defiantly until he smiled faintly and turned away.

Irrationally, her only reaction was to mutter, "I'll never drink another cup of cocoa as long as I live!"

11

A LBIN! WAKE UP!"

"What is it, Mother?" Albin, alarmed, rose on one elbow to peer at the grim face of his wife, leaning over their bed with a lamp in one hand, her hair hanging around her shoulders in plaits.

"Modesty isn't in!"

Albin sighed, yawned, lay back down, and closed his eyes. "She *will* be, Mother. Don't worry."

"But we've been home more than half an hour!"

"That's not too long. Have you forgotten—"

"Albin!"

Dolly stalked the house from window to window until, shortly, the rattle of Judd's buggy was heard pulling into the yard.

Barely restraining herself from yanking her daughter in from the porch, Dolly demanded, as soon as the door closed behind Modesty, "Where do you think you've been, young lady?"

"Mother! You startled me. Where have I been? Why, you know . . . with Judd . . . coming home, of course."

Modesty slipped past her mother's fuming face into the small room she shared with Charity. The whispers and stifled giggles that followed were enough to send Dolly marching into her own room to shake Albin awake and declare in a terrible voice, "That's it! It's clear to be seen—neither of them can be trusted! They'll have me gray and in my grave before my time!"

"Go to sleep, Mother," Albin said mildly. "They're good girls."

"They will be, or my name isn't Dorinda Eustacia Trimble!"

Albin's eyelids flickered, and he turned his face into the pillow.

Grumbling and muttering, Dolly heaved herself into bed to imagine all sorts of improbable scenarios and to work herself into a froth about what she should do about them.

"What would Queen Victoria do?" The ancient queen, of an age to which she was to leave her name as a trademark of propriety and decorum, was the ultimate example in all things, as far as Dolly was concerned.

One final mutter from Albin, and Dolly picked up her ears momentarily to subside at last, thinking she had surely misunderstood what sounded suspiciously like "Cast thy burden on the Lord, and he shall sustain thee."

"Turn over, Albin! You're snoring!"

Morning chores and preparation for church attendance did away with any confrontation between mother and daughters, although the family, knowing her well, shied nervously from Dolly's flaring nostrils and frigid eyes.

After the meeting was dismissed, Modesty slipped to her mother's side and asked, "May I go for a ride with Judd this afternoon?"

"No, you may not," Dolly answered flatly, adding, "We'll talk about that, Miss!"

Modesty, well knowing the seriousness of her mother's tone, was subdued all the way home and through dinner.

In the afternoon while Albin napped and Harmony played outside, Dolly went to the door of her elder daughters' room. "Girls," she said, "I want to talk to you. A mother-daughter talk."

Modest and Charity looked at each other with some trepidation and followed their mother's substantial figure into the front room.

Overflowing the straight-backed chair on which she seemed to reign, Dolly looked at the fair, young faces before her and hardened her heart against their appeal.

"Perhaps you haven't understood the principles your father and I have laid down. Well-brought-up girls don't cavort around with members of the opposite . . . with the male of the species."

The eyes of Modesty and Charity met; nothing could stop the eruption of laughter. It was a bad mistake.

Frost turned to ice. "You, Modesty, will not see Judd Graham for a . . . for a month. And then only if you think you can get in when you are supposed to."

Modesty's mouth opened to protest, but Dolly pressed on. "You, Miss," indicating Charity, "will have nothing whatsoever to do with any member of the opposite . . . gender."

Charity's eyes widened in unbelief. "But . . . why? I'm not a child anymore. You married Dad when you were not much older . . ."

". . . until you learn to conduct yourself," Dolly continued, as though uninterrupted, "less wantonly. You are too impulsive by far, too rash. A . . . a madcap. Thank heavens I didn't name you Prudence!"

Charity groaned. "But Mum—that's the way I am. That's my nature! I'm the one who always tears into her Christmas presents early—don't you remember? I'm the one who dug up the potato seed to see if they had sprouted."

"I don't expect you'll ever be modest or demure," her mother said relentlessly, "but self-control can be learned. And you, Miss, will earn your freedom as you learn it."

Charity's eyes went as gray and dead as the wintering sky outside the window at her side. Her face was as white as her shirtwaist. Without a word she turned and stalked toward the bedroom.

Dolly turned to Modesty and, with a trace of apology, said, "I hope you see the sense of what I'm saying, dear."

When Modesty said nothing, Dolly pushed on. "It's not you so much, dear. Truly, Judd is a fine young man and there is really no problem there. No, it's—"

"It's Marc Szarvas, isn't it, Mum?"

Dolly's eyes shifted.

"But why, Mum? Everyone thinks well of Marc Szarvas."

"Not I! Your father and I wanted that homestead! But that . . . *immigrant*, Lazlo Szarvas, got it! Think of it—an outsider, hardly able to speak the King's English, while my *grandparents* came to the New World. And from England! It's the tower of Babel all over again . . . people jabbering in all sorts of outlandish tongues!"

Modesty's face was a study. "But Mum, doesn't the Bible say something about all believers being one in Christ, that there is no Jew or Greek, bond or free—"

"It also says," Dolly responded promptly, "'Am I my brother's keeper?' If that was good enough for Adam's time, it's good enough for me!" Dolly quoted Scripture as freely as she quoted Queen Victoria.

Modesty opened her mouth to remind her mother that she had used the excuse of the world's first murderer, but Dolly plowed on: "But I *am* my *daughter's* keeper! And I'll keep her from Marc Szarvas if it's the last thing I ever do. She'll thank me someday—you'll see."

"I wouldn't count on it," Modesty said quietly to herself.

Modesty closed the door behind her and looked at her sister on the bed. Charity's despair was beyond tears. She lay on her back, gripping the coverlet with both hands, staring at the ceiling.

"She's crazy," she muttered through stiff lips. "If she thinks—" Charity didn't finish her thought.

"Marc will wait," Modesty said, rubbing her sister's cold hand in hers.

"I don't want to wait." Charity was emotionless, her voice flat. "Marc is the one for me. I know it. Marc knows it. There'll be a way . . . there has to be a way . . ."

Modesty cried helpless tears for those her sister couldn't.

* * *

Charity didn't come out for supper. When Albin asked about her and Modesty made no explanation, he turned questioning eyes on his wife.

"She's sulking, Albin," Dolly said. "But she'll get over it."

Dolly was so strong-willed and so loved to take charge of things that Albin, a peace-loving man, usually went his quiet way, leaving matters in her capable hands. And where his girls were concerned, he felt particularly helpless; they always seemed to be able to twist him around their little fingers, and he found it difficult to reprimand them.

"I hope you know what you're doing," he said now to Dolly, and was only partly convinced when she replied emphatically, "I do, dear. She'll be fine tomorrow—you'll see."

And to his relief, in the morning Charity seemed quite herself. If she were more quiet than usual, he put it down to childishness; she was such a mixture of child and woman. He bent his rawboned frame and kissed her cheek before leaving for the barn. She failed to give her usual rambunctious response, and his eyes sought his wife's. Dolly shook her head warningly, and Albin sighed, patted Charity's shoulder, and left the house.

Charity fixed lunches for herself and Harmony, packing the meat sandwiches and generous slices of Prince Edward cake in the lunch pails. Calling to her small sister, she buckled Harmony into her overshoes, protection against the bitter cold and a precaution against the possibility of snow before the day was over.

Shrugging into her coat, she picked up the pails and her books and turned to go. Modesty watched helplessly.

"Charity," Dolly's voice stopped Charity at the door.

"Turn around!" Dolly said sharply. Charity turned.

"Look at me, Charity," Dolly commanded in exasperated tones. Charity looked.

"Now dear—," Dolly began. But she faltered before her daughter's set face, and the conciliatory words she had been about to say were abandoned. "Don't dally on the way home," she finished lamely, and her face reddened when Charity gave no indication that she had heard or would, indeed, obey.

Finally, with a sigh, Dolly said, "Get on your way, or you'll be late."

Charity closed the door quietly.

"See?" Dolly said to Modesty in a tight voice in the room's silence. "I told you she'd be all right today."

12

THE BURDENED SKY SAGGED LOWER AND LOWER
until, like an overstuffed pillow, it burst its seams and
scattered its feathery load.

From a window in an old log house with a faded
green door, Hubert Runyon peered through a curtain of
snow toward another house, not far away and identical,
except for a faded red door, and watched the smoke curl
from the stovepipe.

"Looky there, Harry," he said, and his brother joined
him.

"I seen snow before, Hu, more than I care to remember."

"Not snow, noodle brain! Smoke—smoke comin'
again from my old house." Hubert's satisfaction was evident in the emotion that quavered his speech.

"Always *was* partial to noodles myself," Harry de-
clared mildly. "Willie's over there cleanin' and paintin',
gettin' ready to move in after the weddin'."

"Seems our cook'll be movin' over there purty soon."

"But she'll still be our cook. And there's somethin'
mighty good cookin' right now." Harry sniffed blissfully,
never quite able to take for granted their good fortune—
blessings—in having their grandniece and her son come
from Manitoba to rescue them from their helplessness and
despair.

"Seems like we saw a pure miracle," Hu marveled, as he often did, thinking, too, about Sarah's entrance into their drab lives. And to think she and Willie Tucker had found happiness in each other!

"Why didn't we pray sooner than we did, Hu?"

"Too ignorant, I guess."

"Speak for yourself!"

And the two old men were off and running, engaged in as fine a spate of repartee as they had enjoyed for weeks.

* * *

In the Jameson household, Abbie also pulled the curtain aside to study the heavily falling snow. Somewhere out there Jamie was hurrying her boys, Corcoran and Cameron, home from school. Not that they couldn't walk today as they usually did. But it was another indication of the care in which Jamie wrapped his new family. It was no surprise to Abbie; Jamie had exhibited those same qualities during the bitter days following Worth's death, when life had caved in on her. Thank God she had recognized it before her stubborn heart had forever enmeshed her in the independent attitude she had projected.

"Thank You, Father, for Jamie," Abbie whispered, knowing her fear of the bush and the smothering blanket of snow had dissipated under her new husband's love and care as surely as spring melts the winter snow.

"Thank you for Papa," small Merry repeated at her mother's side. Abbie turned and caught the little body to her, and together they watched for the arrival of the menfolk in their lives.

Finally—winter and the deep, deep bush held no torments for Abbie.

* * *

Kate dismissed school early, hurrying the children homeward through what promised to be a monumental storm. Walking with those who went her way, she urged them not to dawdle when they eventually turned off to go their own separate ways.

Stamping the snow from her boots, she opened the door to a kitchen fragrant with supper smells. Maggie was pouring water into a teapot! "Bless her!" Kate thought, recognizing a thoughtful gesture on the part of this strong, quiet, lovely, mature woman, about whom she still knew so little. Whatever or whoever she was, she was pure gold.

After hanging up her snow-laden coat and taking the steaming cup, she stepped to the side of the range and said, "It's strange out there!"

Maggie pulled back the calico curtain and peered out at the gloomy sky. "I hope everyone's in," she said. "It's held off so long, and it's so late in coming . . . we'll all be better off to be by our own firesides tonight."

Maggie shivered, and Kate, for some reason, was reminded of the little gold-framed picture and the child whose face had so charmed her and who had never been heard from or seen since.

"It's a time for families to be together—that's for sure," she said thoughtfully. And her thoughts turned to Abram and his small house across the district. She'd feel more secure, somehow, she admitted now, if they were together. Abram was a dose of sunshine on a gloomy day.

He was pressing her for an early wedding. Perhaps it was the loneliness of the day, but "Why wait?" Kate thought now, and the dreariness of the moment lifted at the decision to marry, move into Abram's snug house, and live happily ever after!

"Maggie," she said, turning to her friend suddenly, "could I be ready for a wedding by Christmas?"

* * *

Between the granary and the chicken house, Linn glanced toward the school from which the last child had gone, hurrying through the curtain of snow toward home.

On an impulse, she dropped the pail of mash, glanced

toward the house where her mother read at the side of a reddening heater, and turned quick, impulsive steps up the hill in response to some distant, lingering pull on her heart.

The small building, so central to every life in Wildrose, was more than schoolroom for its children: it was where religious training was received and spiritual truths taught; never locked, the door opened readily.

Stamping the new snow from her feet, Linn closed the door behind her and stood silently in the fading warmth of the great heater while a measure of peace seeped over her bruised spirit. As surely as a birchbark canoe is tossed through boiling rapids, so Linn's frail craft had battered its uncharted way through unfamiliar eddies and whirlpools of the heart.

Rather as a battered craft escapes the grip of powers beyond its control to find itself rudderless in some quiet cove at last, Linn found her way to the corner and the small pump organ. Here she dropped on her knees beside the red velvet, gold-fringed stool to drop anchor as she dropped her head onto her arms.

But her lips would not, or could not, express her mixture of feelings. *God, if You hear wordless cries, hear mine!* But not only did her stubborn lips refuse to voice the help she so desperately needed—additionally, her stubborn heart held in a near death grip an affection that refused to yield to a Heavenly Father's scrutiny.

When she left the room, Linn wondered if she had possibly closed the door on memories that—too bitter to remember—were too sweet to forget.

* * *

Before bedtime the heavy, soft flakes had piled inches deep on every fence post, wrapped every tree and bush in a woolly coat, and erased every stain of man from the face of the earth.

The usual night sounds were muted. Burrowed in their beds, like every other living creature in the bush, people drifted up from sleep to listen to the sound of silence, pull wool quilts a little higher, and strenuously resist any urge or call that might persuade them from their cocoons.

Two feet deep the snow lay when a weak sun, too impotent to do a thing about it, struggled through the thinning atmosphere. Strong men slipped reluctantly from warm beds to cold stoves, blew on feeble coals and coaxed them into flames, adding kindling and opening dampers until heaters glowed red.

Wives shivered their way across linoleum so cold it crackled, to pull a teakettle full of ice to a gradually warming front burner to melt and heat before a face could be washed, a cup of tea made, or cereal cooked.

Children scampered from icy rooms, hopping on cold floors like nimble dancers, twirling like dervishes beside the heater in a futile attempt to warm both back and front. Clothes were hustled to the fireside and donned over the long underwear they had slept in. Hot oatmeal, drowned in creamy milk and laced with brown sugar, promised to "stick to their ribs" for the day ahead and the adventure of breaking trail to the distant schoolhouse.

By Sunday the roads were well opened and the crowd for church was surprisingly good. Red-cheeked and cold-nosed, they laid aside heavy wraps and greeted each other, icy hand gripping icy hand. Hardly anyone noted the humor in one of Brother Victor's hymn selections as they sang lustily:

> *Milk and honey flowing,*
> *Heavenly breezes blowing,*
> *Flowers ever growing,*
> *Fadeless summer day!*

"It wasn't easy getting here today, was it?" the preacher began. Life was like that, he pointed out. The path that had brought them thus far had been fraught with difficulties. "But you have prevailed," he said. And the good news was that the road home would be easier for their having come.

For Linn, the few hundred yards home might as well have been a lifetime: the Christmas wedding of Abram Weatherby and Kate Mason had been announced.

13

SPRINKLING BROWN SUGAR OVER A SMALL bowl of oatmeal in a lackadaisical way, Linn turned to a window crazed with frosty decorations and peered out at the extraordinary beauty of the new day. It was winter at its best. The sun glinted from a billion icy jewels on Mother Nature's snowy breast.

For days now, time had been heavy on Linn's hands; there simply wasn't enough work to keep two women busy in a small house in the dead of winter. Reading materials were limited; newspapers arrived in batches when someone went to the post office to distribute mail all along their homeward route, and Linn supposed she had borrowed every book in every home in Wildrose. And one could only wear so many knitted socks!

There had been a full day or two when they butchered. Most of the meat had been hung from rafters in the granary and would be kept frozen until needed. A few good cuts had been taken to the parsonage and a percentage was canned, which was the only way to have meat—aside from the ubiquitous chicken—in summer months. Canning was a lot of work, but it was gratifying, when company came unexpectedly, to go to the cellar and bring up a sealer of tender meat, ready to heat and serve. No chasing a reluctant chicken . . . no head-chopping . . . no waiting on a hot fire—just heat and eat! What a marvelous boon to housekeeping the glass jar was, with its rubber rings. Such an improvement over making jerky or salting down meat for later consumption!

Every home had its cellar where jars could be kept (hopefully) without freezing. Usually just a large hole cut deep into the earth under the house, it was reached by a trap door in the floor. Here the crop of vegetables, eggs, pickles, jams and jellies, and even nuts from the bush, were stored. Lamp in hand, descent into the dark cavern to the treasure trove was made cautiously indeed.

Every housewife felt a sense of satisfaction in a well-stocked cellar at the summer's end and counted herself fortunate if a supply remained when the chinooks came, the warm winds of spring melted the frozen ground, and gardens produced again. Happy the housewife who came out even on potatoes and meals in a winter season!

Yet never had it all seemed so pointless, so lacking in satisfaction for Linn. And meals, no matter how tempting, were tasteless. Once, stuffing wood into the kitchen range, her face flushed from the heat, she had half-gritted, half-growled the hymn phrase, "How tedious and tasteless the hours," only to turn and find her mother's startled eyes on her.

Now she watched listlessly as Judd added yellow cream to his porridge, stirring it all into a golden mush, and asked, "Did you hear the partridges drumming in the night?"

"Nope. I go to bed to sleep, and that's what I do."

Linn's lips tightened momentarily. Then, "Why don't we go hunting?" she asked, prompted perhaps by the brilliance of the day, as well as her restless, housebound spirit.

"Can't. Supposed to help the Szarvas men with their sawing today. Tomorrow they'll bring their saw here and do our pile, if you remember."

Linn hadn't. But it was the usual pattern—exchanging help on jobs they all had to do.

"Yes, and you be careful, Son!" warned Celia, as she

always did. Hands got numb and awkward in the bitter cold, and accidents happened frequently. More than one household had a man who was missing a fingertip or two.

"I will, Mum. Don't worry," responded Judd, as he always did.

Mother and son smiled at each other, both relieved, somehow, to have said it.

Celia's smile was followed by a sigh as Judd finished his breakfast and got to his feet, stretching his lean, young frame. The responsibilities on him were heavy. But both her children loved the homestead, and neither ever complained of the workload, the deprivation, or the isolation. Of course, they had known nothing else.

But Linn, Celia somehow perceived, had seemed restless of late, not her usual cheerful self. Something was troubling her daughter, and Celia suspected it had to do with her first love. Linn would not give her heart lightly.

As was her custom, Celia kept silent, watched, and prayed.

Linn breathed on the windowpane and scraped the feathery frost with a fingernail, studying the world outside; snow was piled to the windowsills.

"Why don't you get out for a while?" Celia suggested.

Linn turned toward her mother with surprise. "Where in the world would I go?"

Celia had a sudden inspiration. "After partridge, of course. Go by yourself, if your brother can't go. You may not get another day like this for a long time."

Linn was tempted. Even if she didn't find any birds, the tramp through the bush would be exhilarating. "It does sound like fun," she admitted.

"Well, go! I can manage whatever needs to be done . . . there's no need to do any baking today."

"I'll do it!" Linn jumped to her feet and hurried about the few tasks she felt she should do before leaving. She mixed the mash for the chickens and took it out to them, fed the dog, brought turnips up from the cellar, filled the reservoir, and went to get ready.

An old pair of Judd's pants were pulled on and stuffed into the tops of her overshoes. That should keep out the snow. Her bulky jacket was donned over a warm sweater, a scarf knotted around her neck, and a red toque jammed on her head.

"I look like a chickadee!" She laughed at her reflection in the buffet mirror as she reached overhead to carefully remove her father's rifle from the wall.

"It's turnips and potatoes for supper unless you get a partridge!" Celia warned.

Linn grinned, dropped a handful of shells into her pocket, pulled on warm gloves, and stepped out into the brilliant, cold day.

Beyond the yard, crisscrossed by paths, the world stretched in unblemished perfection except for the track that led to the Farley property. The Farley men passed through on occasion, but Linn always managed to evade a confrontation with them, Trapper in particular.

If she had doubted it before, she knew now that Trapper Farley was aware of her feeling—unrequited—for Abram Weatherby. He had watched her reaction Sunday when the jubilant wedding announcement was made (she had visibly started, she knew, and had felt the blood warm her face). Trapp's gaze had been unabashed before her look that warned him to mind his own business.

Already uncomfortable in his presence, she had doubled her efforts to avoid him since that final revealing of her heart.

Linn knew where the partridge were most likely to be found. Crossing the barnyard, the rifle slung loosely in the crook of her arm, she followed the track, stepping along briskly. The squeak of her overshoes on the snow matched the cadence of her heart on this matchless morning. Not very musical, she admitted wryly, but a beginning.

Eventually she plunged from the broken track into the unbroken snow. It was hard going, and she paused from time to time to catch her breath and enjoy her surroundings. Chickadees flew up before her, reluctantly abandoning the seeds they were garnering from the rusty red hips of the wild rose, the only spot of color in the world, it seemed, except for the wide blue sky and her own toque. Tiny paw prints laid down a delicate pattern across snowdrifts, the telltale sign of a mouse emboldened by hunger and beckoned out of its nest by the bright sunshine.

Approaching an open patch of ground quietly, Linn squinted against the glare of sun on snow to see that the snow around a fallen log was disturbed; it was a perfect place to find the fat winter bird.

Linn stuffed her gloves into her pocket, flipped the safety lock on the .22, raised the rifle, and waited. When nothing moved, she picked up a handful of snow, squeezed it into a ball, and flung it toward the log. A startled partridge raised its head.

As she pulled the trigger, a second shot echoed sharply from the bush to her right, the two reports cracking almost simultaneously. The bird was tossed into the air by the double impact, a few feathers scattered wildly, and it fell with a thud into a snowbank.

Into the clearing stepped a man in a gray covert jacket; its drab color had thoroughly hidden him from the bird and the girl. With a few long steps he reached the log and picked up the partridge. His eyes scanned the bush, locating Linn's red toque.

"Come on out," he called.

"Oh no!" moaned Linn. It was Trapper Farley. She sighed, resigning herself to another confrontation.

Trapper Farley watched with an expressionless face as Linn floundered toward him. In front of him, she looked silently at the bird dangling in his hand. "I suppose you think it's yours," she said finally.

"What do *you* think?"

It *was* a neat sidestep; Linn had to admire it.

For the space of a breath Linn considered the possible answers, most of them flippant. She could continue her animosity toward this man or begin a better relationship, and this was the time to do it. But having royally messed up on previous tries, she was cautious.

Linn raised her eyes to Trapp's. His glance was serious enough, but his eyes could have a hidden glint of laughter in their dark blue depths; perhaps it was a reflection of the sun-glittered snow.

Linn's answer was guarded: "I think a gentleman would give it to a lady."

"Not bad!" she thought, proud of her small triumph.

For the space of a breath, Trapper Farley seemed tempted to make something of the "lady." Instead, he held out the bird.

"Where there's one there are bound to be more," Linn said, taking the offering.

"One partridge certainly isn't enough for two tables," Trapp said agreeably.

"I know a likely spot."

Linn started off, Trapper Farley following, fitting his long strides to her shorter ones.

Before another 10 minutes—silent minutes—had passed, they had located two more birds.

"You take the one on the left and I'll get the one on the right," Trapp whispered, and both birds were soon stuffed into the gunnysack he produced.

As they retraced their steps, Linn walked in the tracks of this man who seemed to antagonize her so much, and wondered why.

"Perhaps there's something wrong with me—and men," she sighed to herself. Whatever the reason, she was defensive where this particular man was concerned; perhaps it was because of their ill-timed meeting at her secret hiding place in the bush. Not that subsequent meetings had been any better. It was obvious enough that Berry Lille was enamored of him. As if that mattered.

When, leg-weary and snowy to the knees, they reached the road, Trapp took two partridges from the three in the sack and handed them to Linn.

"A gentleman offers them to a . . . lady," he said, with just enough hesitation to cause Linn to look up at him sharply. Except for a small twitch at the corner of his mouth, however, his face was grave.

Too grave. And Linn's uncertain temper flared. But she managed to respond sweetly. Too sweetly. "I don't know how you'll make one partridge serve three."

"Three?" Trapp's look was wary.

"You, Boyd, Berry."

"A gentleman could give a lady his portion," Trapp said dryly, whereupon Linn whirled and walked off.

It was difficult to be dignified in crunching snow, overshoes slipped in ungainly fashion and balance unsure, and with a couple of partridges flapping against the legs of Judd's old pants.

"Hey, Linn!"

She turned quickly at his call.

Trapper Farley cupped gloved hands to his mouth and his voice carried over the drifts: "By the way—don't you know you're trespassing?"

The warm blood surged into Linn's cold face, and she gasped with outrage.

Flinging herself about, Linn stalked off. The last thing she saw was Trapper Farley's laughing face.

* * *

Celia was pleased to see Linn's red cheeks and glittering eyes, and she concluded the change had done her daughter good. Together they cleaned the birds and set the bulging breasts in a bowl of icy water to await the moment they would be dredged in seasoned flour and fried for supper.

As the three of them sat around the old oak table that night—the heater keeping all but the far corners of the room cozy, cutting into the succulent white meat that was served up with mounds of mashed potatoes, rich brown gravy, and golden turnips—Linn thought about the day, and a gurgle of laughter rose in her throat. When Judd raised curious eyes to her face, she quickly changed the sound into a cough.

Before she fell asleep that night, Linn wondered who had cooked the meat on the Farley table.

14

THE CHRISTMAS PROGRAM, INAPPROPRIATELY but traditionally graced by the term "concert," was slated for the last Friday evening before Christmas.

It was the happiest time of all. Wildrose children, in a state of euphoria, were calmed only slightly by the baths they submitted to a day earlier than usual.

Each child would participate. The small children had short "pieces." The older children gave lengthy and sometimes dramatic readings and recitations and performed in stiff and stilted plays. Musical selections were sprinkled throughout, accompanied by the reedy organ.

Ancient planks, brought from the barn rafters where they had been stored all year, created rows of benches. The rude stage, also made of planks, stretched across sawhorses at the front of the schoolhouse room.

Before the curtain opened on a welcome recitation proudly but nervously delivered, there was standing room only. Those nearest the heater soon found themselves perspiring freely and could do nothing about it. The mingled odors of sweating bodies, wet wool, and homemade soap could not overpower the barn smells that saturated the planks and clung to heavy boots. They were familiar odors and hardly noticed, however, except by the most fastidious.

But through it all the discerning nose caught the heady fragrance of the pine tree—decked with handmade

ornaments and with candleholders clipped strategically to
its boughs—in the front corner of the room, king of all it
surveyed.

Hidden behind the curtain of bedsheets, the prompter
played a vital role. With sibilant whispers she cued the
young performers when they faltered; out front, mothers,
watching tensely, moved their lips silently over lines they
knew word for word.

When at last the oldest pupils gathered self-conscious-
ly onstage to sing "Silent Night," Charity Trimble, although she had practiced obediently with the group, shook
her head and refused to leave her seat. Dolly frowned in
exasperation.

Watching the program, a treat they had not enjoyed
for years, Hubert and Harry found their watery old eyes
beading up more than usual. After missing out on community affairs for so long, to be a part of the life of the district
again was almost more joy than they could handle.

"Lemme use your hankie," Harry urged, as Hubert
wiped his eyes and blew his nose.

"You got your own, you old snifflepoof! I seen Sarah
tuck it in your pocket!"

"But yours is already out, Hu. We'll keep mine for the
next time."

The brothers' distraction over their handkerchief problem made them unaware, briefly, that Marc Szarvas was
working his cautious way past them, apparently heading
for Charity Trimble.

Marc had thoughtfully observed the set shoulders of
the girl and had begun a slow movement toward her. Dolly, engrossed with the performance, failed to notice but
could have done little about it anyway without creating a
scene. And frowns, Dolly was beginning to find, availed
little or nothing with her middle daughter these days.
Charity, face still, would listen patiently to her mother's
sharp instructions, say nothing, and go her way quietly.

Only Albin's warning glance from time to time stemmed the incessant guardianship.

Someone carefully lit the candles on the tree, and the lamps were extinguished. When the candle glow flickered on small, awed, upturned faces, the magic of the moment exceeded anything they would ever know again.

Someone—sly glances around the room usually determined who—had donned the old Santa Claus suit. Amid the merry clashing of harness bells ringing over the wintery landscape and advancing cries of "Merry Christmas!" a figure made his way through the doorway and across the packed house—a minor miracle in itself—and opening a pillowcase, presented each child with a present: tin soldiers for the little boys, knives for the big boys, tiny china boxes painted with vibrant flowers for the little girls, dainty embroidered handkerchiefs for the older girls.

And when they had opened a bag of treats—store-bought hard candy, nuts grown in exotic places, and popcorn pressed into sticky balls—their joy was complete. The only ones more joyous, if possible, were Hubert and Harry.

"Dig out that hankie, Harry!" Hubert commanded, his eyes wet with tears that, prompted by the sight of Simon's happy face, overflowed and ran into the creases of his lined cheeks.

Caught as they were in the crowd, the old men were in a good position to hear the conversation between Marc Szarvas and Charity Trimble as, amid the general pandemonium of dismissal, Marc slid into place at the girl's side. When she slanted a glance at him, he said, "I just wanted you to know—I'm going north after Christmas to work in the timber."

Charity's eyes flickered toward her mother.

"Shall I tell you why?" Marc continued, studying her face, noting the hope that surfaced there. "For money . . . for us."

Despair battled with the hope in the girl's eyes as she lifted them to Marc's face.

"And, Cherry—I've got the logs cut for a house. Father and Billy helped. And when they've seasoned I'll be ready to build. Probably at the end of next summer."

"When I'm 17."

"Good timing, eh?" Marc said with a grin.

"It wouldn't matter—17, 18 . . . 85!" Charity's voice was bitter.

Marc frowned. "You mean . . . ," he said slowly.

"Charity!"

At the sound of her mother's voice, Charity jumped as though she had been struck. And so did Hubert and Harry. At her side and caught up in the drama, the elderly gentlemen were startled at the unexpected harsh command.

Dolly had managed to make her ponderous way through the departing crowd until she stood at the side of the young couple. Anger was written across her face.

"Mrs. Trimble," Marc said, "can we talk for a minute? I should have mentioned this to you before, but—I'm interested in Charity." The words were awkward, but the tone was sincere. Hubert and Harry raised expressive eyebrows at each other.

"You can forget Charity, Marc Szarvas!" Dolly said firmly, and the foreign name sounded like an expletive. "For one thing, she's too young."

"I'm willing to wait," Marc responded stoutly.

Charity had not heard what she needed. "Marc," she began bravely, "waiting won't help. She'll never agree . . . to you and me."

"Of course she will," Marc insisted firmly.

Marc could see no problem that time would not take care of. But riling Dolly's uncertain temper would not help. Discretion might. "The time will go by quickly," he said peaceably.

"Time is not the problem!" There was a rising note of

hysteria in Charity's voice. "Marc—you'll have to stand up to her. Tell her—"

Marc looked at Charity's white face and Dolly's red one and made the decision that satisfied him, calmed Dolly, filled Charity with despair, and catapulted them all into repercussions he couldn't have imagined: "Whatever you say, Mrs. Trimble. Whatever you say."

Dolly shouldered her bulk between the couple and herded her daughter away.

Marc's grin and wink went unseen by a tear-blinded Charity.

As for Hubert and Harry, they looked at each other with consternation. "Hu," Harry said into his brother's hairy ear, "it's prayin' time."

And they turned rheumy eyes in the direction of Sarah and Willie, waiting for them and obviously touching shoulders on purpose. It melted the hearts of the old men.

"We can take credit for that, Harry," Hu whispered back with satisfaction. "And what the good Lord did once, He can do again."

"This playin' Cupid could get to be a habit."

Hu protested. "We're too wrinkled and wobbly for that! No, it's helpin' along what seems like a good thing. That Marc Szarvas is a mighty fine young fella—"

"None better!"

Muttering all this and more, Hubert and Harry submitted their bone-thin arms to the supporting hands of young Simon and tottered toward the door.

* * *

Aside from Charity's anguish, contentment filled the hearts of those who made their way home, calling Christmas wishes to one and all, clutching treasures in mittened hands and trundling across the land—theirs by choice or by birth—a land whose harshness seemed mellowed on this night by a happy time and close friends.

Sleighs and cutters squeaked over snowy roads through a night made memorable by a spectacular display of northern lights shifting silently across the great expanse of sky. No one remained unmoved. As always, the exhibition was so awesome that even the unbelievers among them were tempted to equate it with the supernatural: "The heavens declare the glory of God; and the firmament sheweth his handywork."

Most of the evening's responsibility had been the teacher's. Before dropping off into an exhausted sleep, Kate stepped to the window of her bedroom to take one last look at the land she was beginning to love, knowing that she would view it from a different window ever after. The wedding was scheduled for the following afternoon.

A small light winking from the window of Gabriel Goss's cabin evoked one final thought: "Thank heaven I'll be free of that lecher's odious attention! I wonder who he'll turn his creepy eyes and hands on now!"

✳ ✳ ✳

"Dearly beloved, we are gathered in the sight of God and in the presence of these witnesses"—a few family members, a few friends—"to join in holy matrimony this man and this woman . . ." So read the familiar ceremony as Kate and Abram, along with Maggie Edwards and Marc Szarvas, faced the preacher.

There was no aisle and no runner; Kate stood proudly at Abram's side on a worn rug darkening in spots from the snow that had escaped the broom wielded at the doorstep and now melting in the warmth of the room.

No orange blossom scented the air; the parlor was fragrant with fresh pine, for the Christmas decorations were in place and the small tree stood in the corner.

No one missed the majestic strains of the wedding march; in the hush of the moment, the winter wind played its familiar song at the corner of the house, emphasizing in some way the warmth of the fellowship within.

No stained glass lit the scene; but the Saskatchewan winter sun shone timidly through window and storm window and lit the bride's face with its gentle blessing. Savoring its kiss on her cheek, Kate almost missed her cue.

". . . wilt thou love him, comfort him, obey him, honor and keep him in sickness and in health, and, forsaking all others, keep thee only unto him so long as ye both shall live?"

Firmly, joyously: "I will!"

"Abram, wilt thou have this woman to be thy wedded wife, to live together in the holy estate of matrimony? Wilt thou love her, comfort her, honor and keep her, in sickness and in health, and, forsaking all others, keep thee only unto her so long as ye both shall live?"

And why shouldn't he promptly promise, "I will"?

Brother Victor ceremoniously concluded, "Forasmuch as Kate and Abram have consented together in holy wedlock and have witnessed the same before God and this company, I pronounce they are husband and wife, in the name of the Father, and of the Son, and of the Holy Spirit. Those whom God hath joined together, let not man put asunder!"

And family and friends gathered around amid smiles and tears after the groom had "saluted" the bride.

Following the serving of Maggie's rich, dark fruitcake, the bride and groom drove away in his cutter to the waves and best wishes of those who were assembled on the steps, hugging themselves against the cold.

As they flew over the frozen roads, Abram held Kate close and congratulated himself on his good luck: young, strong, with a farm and a house of his own, and now a wife of his choice—an outstanding catch. Life looked good.

If, when they passed the dark schoolhouse, memories stirred and an uneasy picture of a sensitive face and trusting eyes rose before him, Abram thrust it from him. If a brief thought touched his mind that Linn Graham may not have interpreted his . . . attentions casually on that rain-wrapped night not too long ago, he scoffed at the idea and put the whole episode into a file—a bulky file—marked "Plans that didn't pan out."

* * *

Closing the door to the henhouse, Linn caught the sound of a rig passing on the schoolhouse road and as it flashed over the crest of the hill, recognized it for Abram Weatherby's. The groom was taking his bride to her new home.

In spite of recent victories, a pang of bitterness welled up in Linn's heart, and she heartily regretted having accepted Trapper Farley's invitation to go with him to the shivaree.

Already planning to plead a headache if Judd should ask her to go, Linn had been persuaded when Trapp had stopped his horse earlier in the day and called to her as she crossed the yard. He looked down at her with an expression on his face she couldn't quite fathom.

But his voice was casual: "What about the shivaree, Linn?"

Startled, she asked, "What—what do you mean?"

"I mean," he said deliberately, "what are you going to do about it?"

"Nothing. Why should I?"

"Isn't that cowardly?" Trapp's eyes were their darkest blue and his gaze was straight.

Linn shifted her eyes. "What could you possibly know about it?" she asked angrily, knowing he knew enough.

And it was "Enough," he answered. "Enough to know you need to face the fact of Abram's marriage and go on from there. Or," he added with gentle humor, "am I trespassing again?"

"Yes! No. But why? Why do you do it?"

"Can't a person want to be a good neighbor? Or even a friend?"

"But why should you want to go to a shivaree? And for people you hardly know?"

Trapp grinned, his white teeth flashing in his north woods-darkened face. "That's easy—anything to break the boredom."

Even for people accustomed to the long winters, the confinement at times was oppressive. Trapp waited for Linn's answer. It was slow in coming.

"Perhaps you're right," she finally admitted. "Perhaps I have been acting like a coward. Funny though—I thought all the time I was being . . . brave. I'll do it! I'll go!"

Now she regretted the decision, and her mind skittered around like a mouse in a trap, seeking some way out.

But when Trapp's cutter pulled into the yard, she was dressed and ready; she even managed to set her toque at a jaunty angle on her lively, gold-streaked hair.

Trapp tucked the robe around her and Linn settled back enjoying, in spite of herself, the beauty of the night. The Christmas moon "gave the lustre of mid-day to objects below" and laid a silvery path from the sky across the wide expanse of snow to the cutter, moving with them until it seemed to be a bright ribbon attached to the sleigh runners.

"A light that shineth in a dark place," Trapp Farley said quietly. But not too quietly to be heard above the movement of the cutter over the snow. "Until the day dawn, and the day star arise in your hearts," he concluded.

Dismayed, Linn could only turn and look at him.

"Do you think it might?" he asked, his gaze fixed on the horse's ears.

"It might what?" she asked, bewildered.

"Arise in your heart—the day star."

But Linn was too taken aback to respond sensibly. Her mumble was lost in the syncopation of the trotting hooves and the jingling of the harness.

For Linn, Scripture and prayer were relegated to her mother and to Brother Victor, or for mealtimes and bedtimes. Or, she admitted now, for desperate moments. That Trapper Farley should take it seriously . . .

When they pulled into the Weatherby yard and joined the small group clustered behind the granary, Trapp touched Linn's elbow and whispered, "Chin up!"

Linn wasn't sure her teeth-chattering was due to excitement, cold, or nervousness. Then they were caught up in the raucous din of the shivaree, beating their pie tins and tin cans, sweeping with the crowd into the house.

The bride and groom, with self-conscious smiles, greeted their uninvited but expected guests and served the refreshments they "just happened" to have ready. Linn stood with the others in the midst of the confusion and heard the laughing and teasing. All around were indications of a woman's touch: pictures arranged on log walls that had been freshly whitewashed, glassware shining on the sideboard, new towels hanging beside the washstand, an embroidered tablecloth. And the woman responsible for it stood by her husband with happy face and shining eyes.

"And to think I called her a little brown wren!" Linn recalled somewhat shamefacedly.

Just when Linn wasn't sure how much more she could stand, when her lips were stiff with her smiling, Trapper Farley tipped his head in the direction of the door, and they made their escape. Linn stumbled toward the cutter.

"Get in," Trapp said tersely, and she did.

Slapping the reins on the mare's back, Trapp hurried the rig out of the yard and down the road. "Are you sure you care all that much?" he asked finally.

It was the question Linn had been asking herself.

"Why don't you let go of it?" he added.

Linn almost flared to anger. But she had a feeling that Trapper Farley was near to excising the wound.

"Tell me you love him," Trapper Farley probed deeper.

Linn was silent.

"Go on—say it."

Linn opened her mouth to speak and found she could not. Instead, a laugh, free and easy, formed in her throat, and her spirits soared as she let it go.

"I can't say it," she said, surprised. "Not any more."

Trapper Farley drew a great breath of air into his lungs and expelled it with a long sigh; it wreathed his head in a white cloud and dissipated, left behind on the winter road.

15

JANUARY CAME AND WENT, A WHITE BLUR. THE
winter sky seemed never to tire of weaving intricate
lace, each stitch unique and fragile. Winter winds flung it
about, and the winter sun, exerting her feeble influence,
gently pressed it onto the earth in the soft, demure folds of
an exquisite shawl.

In the same way that rabbits and certain small rodents
dig out after storms, so humans crawled out of their bur-
rows with the same regularity, patiently making new paths
to outhouses, barns, wells, henhouses, and haystacks, only
to have it snow again and the whole thing to do over.

Ash heaps grew larger as woodpiles grew smaller.
Manure piles expanded as haystacks diminished. Jars full
of color and flavor were brought from cellars and returned
empty to the shelves.

It was the time of stillness. Gone the restless stirrings
in the treetops, gone the dancing leaves. There was no
trembling butterfly, no drifting cloud of dandelion seed.
No blowing grass, no bending grain. Never a creeping bug
or scurrying ant. Plow and harrow and binder stirred no
dust in silent fields. No ripple spread from webbed feet in
slough or lake. The wind blew, and if it were not for the
loose snow it riffled, the horses' manes and tails it tossed,
and the smoke it carried away, you could hardly tell.

It was the time of silence. No meadowlark warbled

116

from snow-capped fence post. No grasshopper chirped, no frog croaked, no bee buzzed, and no mosquito hummed. Not a fly tormented horse or housewife. The chicken's cackle and the calf's bawl were muffled by sturdy hen-house and barn. Any drop melting from a fire-warmed roof was caught at the eave and bonded into an icicle before its small splash could break the vacuum of silence.

It was a colorless time. Gone the flashing breast of red robin and the blue wing of the jay. There was no blush of dusky wild rose, dainty bluebell, or flamboyant tiger lily. The green shroud of the bush vanished. No succulent fruit hung ripe and brilliant. The golden-stubbled fields had disappeared along with the purple-topped thistles and yellow dandelions that invaded them.

The smells of the bushland vanished. Gone the dainty scent of flowers, the woodsy aroma of fresh leaves and damp leaf mold. And gone the potpourri of grass, goldenrod and roses, crushed strawberries, rain-drenched fields, cultivated earth, and thunderstorms. All outdoors became an odorless void. The nostrils were stung by the bitter cold, and the lungs ached with it; but it was bereft of bouquet.

Indoors was another matter. Windows were not opened from the beginning of the season until the advent of spring's enticing breezes and chinooks. Doors opened only wide enough and long enough for the inhabitants of the house to slip in and out. Cooking odors impregnated the very walls. Because bathing was indulged in but once a week, the hot air billowing from the potbellied heaters was thick with body odors. Cats and dogs added to the pungency, as did barn boots, kept inside by the door for the sake of feet that would be thrust into them at intervals.

But the refreshing tang of poplar and spruce, piled into wood boxes and chunked into heaters and kitchen ranges, cleansed the atmosphere. Smoke, escaping from the opened stove or seeping into a room because of a faulty damper, had the same effect. Fresh-baked bread was a heady fragrance.

Before the year's first month had ended, Kate Mason Weatherby had reason to suspect she was pregnant. And it was confirmed by the winter smells. Children crowded into the small schoolroom, smacked their mittens on the side of the stove to dislodge the icy particles that clung to them, laid them under the heater to dry—and the wet-wool smell caused Kate's stomach to heave. The smelly drops sizzled and skittered across the heater's surface after morning recess, lunchtime, and afternoon recess, with fearful consequences. Bending over sweaty young bodies became an ordeal; horsehairs clinging to bareback riders brought an effluvium that sickened Kate.

She kept her suspicions to herself, at first. Frankly, she was a little dismayed to be having a baby so soon and wondered uneasily about Abram's reaction. She and Abram were, she admitted, strangers to each other in many ways—their courtship had been so brief. Beyond the fact that Abram was fun-loving, gregarious, and genial, her husband's characteristics were still unknown to her.

When he arrived one afternoon to take her home, Kate was fastening the buckles on the overshoes of the smallest Victor child, overshoes that had been too close to the heat; the softened rubber was hot to the touch and almost sticky. As Kate rose to her feet, giving a helping hand to the scarf-swaddled child, she swayed momentarily. Abram thought at first she had lost her balance. But catching sight of her white face he stepped to her side, supported her, and exclaimed, "Katy—what's wrong?"

There was no use pretending. Kate fell into his arms, making silent puddles of tears on his shoulder. He pulled away from her, peering anxiously into her face. "What is it?" he demanded anxiously. "What's happened?"

"*You're* what happened!" Kate said, half vexed, half laughing, making an attempt to dry her eyes.

"Me? Sweetheart—I'm sorry—"

Whereupon Kate burst into a fresh wail, burying her face in Abram's mackinaw again.

Struggling between concern, annoyance, and curiosity, Abram sat down, pulled Kate down beside him, and said, "Now, are you going to tell me?"

"Abram . . . I think I may be . . . having a baby."

Abram was, perhaps, just a moment too long in responding. When he did it was with a heartiness that confirmed Kate's fears; he wasn't all that pleased.

"A baby! How about that!"

Kate needed reassurance. "Is it all right? I mean, really all right?"

"Silly! It's wonderful! I was just surprised for a moment."

"And you were going to apologize!" Kate quavered, and when Abram laughed, she joined in shakily.

"So when will the great day be?" Abram asked as he tucked the robe around his wife and climbed into the cutter beside her.

"Just about a year from the time we met," Kate said ruefully.

"If it's a girl we can call her Annie, for anniversary," Abram said with his usual good humor, and Kate found herself laughing at him, as she so often did.

* * *

It was a February to remember—or to forget as quickly as possible.

Firesides were small sanctuaries from the intense cold that crept from a frozen world into houses where nail heads frosted and water pails froze solid overnight.

The smallest variation in the routine of long, isolated days took on great importance: a rare visitor, mail dropped off by a passerby, the loan of a book. Meals, always simple, became high points. Summer-canned juices were opened, sweetened, and thickened into a sort of fruit soup, served with cream so thick it plopped from the pitcher—a dish fit for a king. Despite prickly cases, hazelnuts were cracked and were nuttier and sweeter for the waiting.

Children invented games: checkers with buttons from mother's button box, jigsaw puzzles from magazine pictures pasted onto cardboard and cut into pieces. Every book was read and read again; Wildrose children were good readers. Wool was knitted into strange and lumpy shapes by small fingers, raveled, and knit again. Paper dolls were cut from catalogs, along with the clothes in which to dress them.

Perhaps because of the tedium, church services were unusually well-attended. And it was at Sunday morning service Linn saw Trapper Farley again, the first since the night of the shivaree, when he had faced her with her foolish feelings for Abram Weatherby and she had undergone a purging of some sort.

Now, thinking of Abram, Linn could wonder, "How could I have been so naive?" (But how could he have been so false?)

Brother Victor, preaching his sermon on keeping the Sabbath day holy, ruefully and humorously admitted to himself that the same message, delivered in the balmy days of summer—when his flock was inclined to overlook the biblical injunction—would not have aroused such a hearty flurry of amens.

Trapp's eyes met Linn's across the room. She flushed, but her gaze was held by his steady one. That Trapp saw a shadow of embarrassment, a question in her eyes, Linn never knew. But when his eyes crinkled slightly and his lips softened in a hint of a smile, a warmth flooded her.

"Heavenly sunshine," she sang with the others, with true fervor.

And when on Monday Trapp's cutter stopped at her door and he knocked, entering the small kitchen to smile at her openly and suggest that she put on her coat and accompany him to Meridian, she turned without hesitation to call, "Mum, I'm going out. Trapper Farley is here. He's going to Meridian."

"Fine, dear," Celia responded from the other room and the fireside. "Get the supply list and my coin purse."

The horse and cutter flew over the snow-packed roads, the harness keeping musical accompaniment. Trapper Farley's eyes, usually so dark a blue, glinted like sapphire chips. Catching Linn's eyes upon him, he flashed her a grin. Linn's responding smile was spontaneous.

Charity Trimble, on a lonely walk along a lonely road, heard the laughter as the cutter flashed past and wondered if she would ever make such a happy sound again.

* * *

Charity escaped the house, with its confinement and close quarters, whenever she could. Usually it was just to tramp the winter world by herself. More than once her wanderings took her past the Runyon farm. Harry and Hubert, peering out in response to the barking of young Simon's dog Scratch, studied the lonely figure on her aimless walk, with her bent head and drooping shoulders, and, recalling the strange conversation they had overheard at the Christmas program, cast meaningful glances at each other.

"Don't look like we got an answer to our prayer, Harry," Hu sighed. "Look at her, draggin' along, the picture of misery."

"O ye of little faith!" Harry quoted feelingly as he turned from the window to creak his way to his chair, followed by his brother. Together they picked up Bibles belonging, in earlier, happier days, to Bessie and Virgie.

After fumbling his stiff fingers through the pages a while, Hu asked, "Whereabouts you figure we oughta start lookin'?"

"Corinthimums," Harry said promptly. "Here—I got it marked. See, Hu, it says if we've got faith, we can remove mountains. C'mon, Hu, we need to memorize this."

"I don't know, Harry," Hu grumbled. "Why can't we just say 'Prayer changes things' like ever'body else?"

"Are you sure that's a proper verse, Hu?" Harry questioned suspiciously.

"No," Hu admitted, "but it sure sounds good to me."

And so they continued to be occupied for the afternoon, focusing as best they knew how on the dilemma of young Charity Trimble, who had presently chosen to follow a familiar path to the Edwards place.

Maggie had been Charity's Sunday School teacher for several years. Always the same—cheerful, courteous, dignified, and caring—Maggie had earned the respect and love of Charity. Now, if Maggie wondered about the girl's restlessness, she never asked, but offered a cup of tea and a warm hug whenever Charity, with a haunted look about her, slipped into the security and warmth of the Edwards' kitchen.

If on occasion the lonely girl exchanged glances with Gabriel Goss, John's hired man, it was done without the scrutiny of an overly careful mother or the worry of a caring friend. Gabe Goss was, after all, much too old for serious consideration of a young woman the age of Charity Trimble.

That Charity was indeed a young woman and no child Maggie perceived—and wondered uneasily if Dolly Trimble was as aware of the girl's maturity as she ought to be.

Dolly was aware of her daughter's visits to Maggie and had deep-seated resentment to contend with; she could in all honesty, however, find no reason to forbid the contact.

"There's something about that woman . . . ," she fretted to Albin, "and I can't figure out what it is."

"Oh, Mother," Albin began wearily. "Maggie and John are above reproach."

"But who are they? And where did they come from?—I tell you, Albin, there's something fishy going on."

"They're from B.C.," Albin explained patiently. "Like

all of us, they wanted a new frontier, and it brought them to Wildrose."

Dolly sniffed. "She doesn't dress one bit like Queen Victoria . . . those colors she uses—wine red, cadet—what sort of name is that for a color, anyway? And that feather, Albin—ostrich, if I know my feathers! The good Queen—"

"Twenty-fourth of May, the Queen's birthday . . . ," screeched Harmony, prancing through the room. When her mother turned scandalized eyes in her direction, the child changed speed and escaped the scolding she knew was coming. And in the process she diverted Dolly from her tirade against Maggie Edwards.

The truth was, Dolly was suffering the pangs of conscience; she knew she had sacrificed her daughter's confidences. To imagine she was sharing them with Maggie Edwards was almost more than she could bear.

Apologizing was not in Dolly's makeup. And to "mend fence" with Charity meant softening her stand against Marc Szarvas. Dolly almost wished she had never got herself entangled in a standoff over that particular young man. To think that Charity would become so adamant! Dolly had supposed the child would subside after a pout or two, and that would have been that.

Was it worth the tug-of-war? Dolly thought it was.

16

THOUGH IT SEEMED IT WOULD NEVER HAPPEN, a day came, as it always has and always will as long as the earth remains, when warm chinooks blew, and the north wind, spent and chastened, whimpered a few times and withdrew. Eventually, as it always had and always will as long as the earth remains, it would sweep back, refreshed and renewed, swollen with power and furious at the interruption. But that would be several wonderful months distant.

Water dripped from eaves until roofs gleamed, wetly naked. Melted snow ran from the bottoms of shrinking drifts, and snowbanks settled silently earthward. A hundred and more rivulets ran down inclines to form sloughs in every hollow, and brisk breezes rippled them like miniature oceans.

As she did every spring, Linn judged the time to be right, pulled on rubber boots, slung a soft sweater of Celia's winter knitting over her shoulders, and searched the woods until she found it: the harbinger of spring in the bush.

Palely purple it was and as soft as the inside of a baby rabbit's ear. Lovely and alone it grew, cradled in wet remnants of snow in a hidden recess.

Crouching over it, almost crooning in her delight at having found it, Linn cupped the crocus in her hands. After a long winter of no fresh, living thing, the sign of new life was nothing short of a miracle.

This year it meant more than "The flowers appear on the earth; the time of the singing of birds is come." This year it meant—surely and certainly—"To every thing there is a season, and a time to every purpose under the heaven."

Having experienced "a time to weep," could it now be "a time to laugh"? Remembering "a time to lose," was it now "a time to get," "a time to keep," "a time to love"?

Absorbed with the beautiful thing, Linn didn't hear the footsteps muted by soggy ground. Trapper Farley stopped and watched her delight in the small, elusive blossom.

At the snap of a twig, she looked up at him. Eyes still tender, "Look," she said softly, willing to share the special moment, the special meaning.

Trapp's reaching hand found a small warm one waiting. As sweet in her own way as the flower, she raised her face to him and lifted, with the gentle pressure of his grip, to stand before him, lost in the dark eyes looking down on her, and drawn by the enticing curve of his handsome lips.

As a flower bends in the breezes of spring, Linn leaned toward the man who, like the warm spring sun, drew her until his mouth met hers. As sweetly as bee and blossom kiss, so he kissed her. With the mild winds teasing about them, and with the tender flower of promise nodding at their feet, he kissed her.

Finally, swaying back to lean against a sap-touched poplar, breathing shallowly, she stared at him with wide eyes.

"It was the crocus," he said. "The first crocus of the year affects me like this."

His tone was grave enough, but there was that familiar humor—once so antagonizing and now so endearing—that played around his mouth and gentled his eyes.

Then together they knelt in the damp earth beside the sturdy emissary of spring, that messenger that signified the life and hope unfolding across the length and breadth of the bush.

And when they turned to go, it seemed important, somehow, to leave it there, blooming . . .

* * *

When she had come, a stranger, to Wildrose to teach, Kate had fallen in love with the bush as it had welcomed her so generously in the fall of the year. As for winter, it had been spent in a cozy home, warmed by love. The months had slipped away in a happy dream.

Wildrose was a parkland in the spring.

Accustomed to rising early all week, Kate automatically awoke at the same hour on weekends, usually grateful that she could snuggle down for another hour or so. But with the advent of spring there was a freshness about the day, an anticipation, and she was filled with eagerness to be a part of it, hating to miss any of it, and was up early, and outside.

Across the greening yard, Abram drove the cows through dew-drenched new growth; the cowbell beat a tinny tune. And from bush and meadow rose a sound that thrilled all heaven and most hearts. For there is really nothing to compare with spring in the bush, with its multitudes of birds expressing their pleasure in the new day by filling the endless miles of clear sky with incredible variations of sound and flashes of color. They seemed to usher in the warm weather, as if, by the magic of their song, they whistled up soft winds and teased the earth into waking and responding with a melody all its own.

Kate placed her hands on her stomach, strangely at one with the burgeoning land. The swelling life within and without stirred an earthly kinship.

She reached over the edge of the porch to the lilac bush that some early homesteader had planted, checking the baby-green shoots and tender buds. Soon, she thought, the lovely wildrose would unfold its beauty and fragrance over the world from a thousand and more bushes. Fancy breathing in and finding it pure perfume!

* * *

Marc Szarvas, back from the north woods and with money jingling in his pocket, made his eager way toward the schoolhouse and Charity.

With the wages he had earned he could proceed with the building of his cabin on the vacant homestead next to his parents' place. With his father's help he could build some simple chairs and stools, a table, cupboard, and washstand; he could purchase windows, hardware, stovepipes, and a range. Marc had his heart set on the Acme Royal Range and studied the catalog, memorizing its advantages: "This $24.92 stove is the equal of any range on the market, regardless of price; combines every improvement of every high-grade range made, with the defects of none."

With its "Full-scale Oven, Duplex Grate, Cut Tops and Centers, Porcelain-lined Reservoir, Oven Door Kicker, Large Fire Box, Large Flues, Bailed Ash Pan, Slide Hearth Plate, and Latest and Handsomest Rococo Design," Marc was certain it would bring delight to Charity's heart.

Time, Marc thought, was all he needed, and he had plenty of that! He would wait. Would Charity? With a need to see her, reassure her, finalize their hopes and plans, he hurried his pace.

Standing impatiently by the school fence, Marc watched the children pour from the doorway, eager for the freedom they had anticipated for so many housebound months. Leaping and cavorting, they scattered from the steps. His own heart leaped when Charity appeared.

The months had changed her; there was no spring in her movements, no girlish leap into life. But when she saw him she hurried her step.

"Marc! When did you get back?"

"Just yesterday."

"So why did you wait so long to come see me?" Charity laughed, and Marc with her.

When she realized Marc was going to walk home with her, her laughter stilled. "I don't know if that's a good idea . . ."

Marc tipped his hat back and scratched his head in a puzzled fashion. "I don't know why *not*, goosey!"

"Harmony," Charity said, turning to her sister, "walk on ahead. But don't tell Mum that Marc is walking me home."

When Marc gave Charity the small bottle of *Creme Pour Peau Seche* with its promise to "protect, soften, and moisturize dry, chapped skin," her delight was obvious, but now he sensed a certain restraint in her manner. Marc turned thoughtful.

"Charity," he said seriously, "don't change on me . . . don't ever change."

"I'm not the one who has changed," she said, giving him a slanting glance.

"Well, *I* certainly haven't!" he maintained stoutly.

Mercurial as always, Charity dropped the subject and began chattering in her usual manner. Half-listening, Marc faced the fact that Charity really knew little or nothing of his plans for them. Her impulsiveness and his masculinity were a flammable combination. Marc had deliberately chosen what to him seemed the wise way: keep the relationship casual, thus curbing Charity's ardency and eliminating temptations that would inevitably follow.

There was no weakness in Marc's decision-only strength. The uselessness of contending with Dolly—Charity was not of age, she was living at home, she was indeed young—lent patience to an already patient man.

This was not the time to disclose his depth of feeling to her. But it was hard . . . so hard. So Marc teased and

laughed in his usual lighthearted way with her until finally, "This is as far as you better come," she said uneasily.

Marc stiffened. He had no intention of being surrepti-
tious where his relationship with Charity was concerned;
neither did he grasp the inflexibility of Dolly's will.

"Marc! Mum will be furious!"

"I'll talk to her," Marc said placatingly, and walked on.
Beside him Charity dragged her feet, her eyes apprehensive.

Dolly was waiting. Having forced from Harmony the
reason for Charity's delay, she now stood, grim-faced, on
the steps.

"Go to your room, Miss!" she commanded.

"But Mum—"

"March!" Dolly pointed a stiff finger, and Charity,
looking sick, turned to go.

"Wait a minute," Marc said in a surprisingly com-
manding tone. "We've done nothing wrong."

Dolly crossed her arms on her high, firm bosom, and
spoke in a voice equally high and equally firm. "Why are
you so stubbornly persistent? Forget my daughter, Marc
Szarvas! She isn't for you. She's my responsibility, and I in-
tend to protect her—If not from you, then from herself."

Charity, white as an eggshell, gave a cry, and Marc's
brow darkened. "You've insulted both of us!" he exclaimed.

Nevertheless, it was Dolly who won. Taking Charity
by the arm, she propelled her toward the house. "I forbid
her to see you again! Do I make myself clear?"

Charity's eyes clung to Marc's, sick and ashamed, and
it broke his heart. In spite of Dolly's rigid bulk, he stepped
to the girl's side and said, "I understand. But when she's
18 I'll be back."

Charity was weeping, shaking her head.

"Eighteen," Marc repeated. "She'll be her own woman
then, and I'll be back." And he couldn't understand the tri-

umph in Dolly's face as she propelled her daughter toward the door, nor the plea in Charity's.

Watching helplessly, Marc gritted his teeth. He could only wait. If he ran off with her, Dolly would have the law on him. And he wanted it to be right, for Charity's sake.

His schedule . . . his plans . . . he would cling to them and work toward their eventual fulfillment. For now it was all he had.

But Charity knew nothing of Marc's schedule and little of his plans. The hope in her eyes—that he would do something *now*—turned to unbelief as he turned away and to black anger when he walked from the yard. Snatching her arm from Dolly's grip, Charity stalked into the house.

Dolly heaved a sigh of relief. "Let him wait," she exulted, knowing her impetuous daughter well. "*She* certainly won't. There's got to be someone more . . . suitable than that Marc Szarvas!"

17

HARMONY'S COUPLET CONCERNING THE queen's birthday was chanted by children all across the Territories. The only celebration of the old monarch's birthday was that, by tradition, they took off their long underwear. But that was momentous!

What exquisite freedom to run without that bulky garment hampering active bodies and legs!—to become overheated without suffering cloying perspiration under fleece lining from wrist to throat to ankle. What satisfaction—for girls whose legs had been embarrassingly disfigured for months by lumpy wrapping and baggy knees—to expose discreet glimpses of shapely limbs!

What pleasure to see 100 or more blackbirds sweep, as on a single wing, to settle on reeds and rushes, flaunting their red badges—to hear the gray squirrel scold from a greening bough, his tail hoisted rakishly over his back!

The treasures to rediscover were endless: the old playhouse in the birches, the little red wagon, rustier than they had remembered; the first violet; a buttercup to be plucked and held under the chin and the golden reflection marveled at.

The binder on every farm was host to a family of wrens. With busy persistence, they filled the twine boxes with twigs and grass and darted in and out of their private quarters through the tiny aperture that would, come harvesttime, dispense the twine.

Pigs, so repulsive later on, entered the world pink and darling. The graceless turkey was adorable when it pecked its way from the egg. Baby chicks, held in small hands, felt like balls of dandelion seed, light and soft and formless. Kittens mewed from under the porch and in hidden recesses of the haymow. Broody hens pecked wickedly at curious, extended hands. The newborn calf, unsteady on its feet, wound its rough tongue around childish fingers.

Even the garden had its delights to soften the pain of work: earth, damp and black, sensuous to bare feet that had so recently clumped in heavy overshoes; precise rows of delicate green growth, magically appearing where infinitesimal seeds had been scattered just a few days before; the curling leaves of the unfolding rhubarb; wriggling worms in a spadeful of fresh-turned soil (where had they been all winter?). There were no casual responses to spring in Wildrose.

School was over for the year. Report cards were ready for distribution. And they would be handed out at the annual picnic that brought the district together in one glorious celebration of winter's demise.

Sponsored by the Wildrose Sunday School, the picnic was traditionally held at Puddle Lake. It started early in the day and ran until late afternoon, when evening chores called. There were games, races, swimming for those who would brave the still-cold water—and best of all, hours of visiting, catching up on news that had been tucked away all winter. From all across the district they would come, entire families, for the last idle hours before plunging into the urgency of the summer schedule.

At noon all activities would cease and everyone would gather around the long tables—boards set up on sawhorses—where every taste treat imaginable awaited and each cook had her specialty. Underneath the tables waited freezers of homemade ice cream.

By dusk everyone was gone but lingerers and lovers.

More fun was possible after twilight than before, according to some, and they bided their time until the wagons had creaked off and, with them, the stern eyes of parents and preacher and the taunts of sharp-eyed and sassy-tongued children.

Judd Graham and his rig were among the first to pull into the shade of the poplars at the lakeside; others followed in quick succession. Linn, looking cool and vibrant in a white dress traced with green, helped Celia—who had been persuaded to come along for the fellowship with dear friends— from the wagon to a comfortable place under the trees.

Casually, Linn checked the gathering rigs and warmed with pleasure when the Farley buggy rolled in. Trapper and Boyd, "strong, dark, and handsome," waved to the assembled group, but Trapp's eyes sought out Linn.

It was the only invitation Linn needed. With a light step she went to meet him, knowing that her arrogant spirit had finally kissed its resistance good-bye.

But it hadn't happened overnight. There was, about Linn's and Trapp's relationship, a gentleness. Missing was the pulsing pressure Linn had felt with Abram Weatherby. Sometimes she suspected Trapp was deliberately allowing space for their budding intimacy to develop naturally, giving her time to embrace trustingly what he had to give.

They had walked together on a Sunday afternoon. Linn introduced Trapp to her favorite places: the beds where spring flowers bloomed, the berry bushes sifting their petals like snow, the tussocky sloughs.

He had directed their steps, that spring day, through the woods to his place. There he had given her a tour, with an obvious sense of satisfaction in what had been accomplished. The fields stretched in neatly plowed and sowed rows, piglets squealed in rebuilt pens, chicks scurried to the call of the mother hen, and a garden was greening nicely.

But it was the log house he drew to her attention.

"Well, what do you think?" he asked after they had stepped inside.

The sunlight through the window fell over Linn's face and hair, which, her mirror told her daily, retained its sun-streaked appearance year round. When she looked up, Trapp, obviously seeing the similarity in her eyes (here, too, a strange blend of colors—mossy green and brown shot with golden shafts), said, "I suppose the term is hazel," and smiled as his finger touched her cheek briefly, lightly. Linn felt he was taking her to a place . . . a depth she hadn't known before, and by a safe route. Suddenly she was filled with a passionate gratitude for his consideration.

When Trapp's hand fell away from her cheek, he said, rather abruptly, "The house, how does it look to you . . . now?"

The walls gleamed white; the newly laid linoleum was bright; the simple furniture was comfortably arranged.

Linn was not surprised at the extra touches: the blackened stovetop and the shining nickel, the crisply ironed curtains, a bowl of lilacs—not things a man would have time for.

The wisp of a familiar hurt uncurled itself in Linn's subconscious mind (where it had long lain, she supposed), and she said, with a touch of sharpness, "Don't tell me you managed all this by yourself."

"Oh, I have help," Trapp said, and she felt his eyes on her face. When she turned away, shoulders stiff, he followed silently.

Now, with the laughter and confusion of the picnic crowd around them, Linn believed she saw something special in Trapper Farley's dark eyes, and the day came alive for her.

Trapp took her hand and looped it through his arm, and they turned their steps toward the meadow and the activities there. Abram Weatherby was organizing the children's races, obviously at Brother Victor's request, and he looked rather impatient and already hot and sweaty.

Further on, a ball game was about to begin; all the usual young men were there choosing sides. A bevy of girls, like a bouquet of spring flowers, bloomed on a grassy bank. Like blossoms bending in the breeze, they leaned toward each other, whispering, casting speculative glances toward the male figures on display for their benefit. Never did men flex muscles any more deliberately, leap higher, or run swifter. And it was all noted and appreciated. Linn joined her friends, and Trapper Farley was hailed as umpire.

As the day wore on, Celia Graham, never strong these days, felt the need of rest. Linn fixed a comfortable spot in the shade, settled her mother there, and decided to take her home as the day cooled. Regretfully, she realized it would mean she couldn't spend the evening with Trapp. She had responded so happily to his invitation and had anticipated being with him and the other couples at the lakeside under the summer moon.

"I'll be fine, dear," Celia insisted, not wanting to interfere with her daughter's plans or her son's. Judd had sprinted off to Modesty's side with an eagerness that had tightened Dolly Trimble's already prunelike lips, and Celia wished the young couple well.

But Linn noted the perspiration on her mother's brow and the lack of color in her face. "I know, Mum," she said gently. "Just rest awhile." Celia put her head back and closed her eyes.

Linn looked around for Trapp to tell him she would be taking her mother home rather than sending her with a neighbor, as originally planned.

She could see no sign of the figure her eyes searched for—lithely muscled, brown, and vigorously healthy. But she did catch a glimpse of a pink dress disappearing into the bush at the meadow's edge.

One glimpse, and like an arrow from a well-aimed

bow the suspicion struck and quivered: Berry Lille—lovely in pink today, cool and remote, drifting quietly among the crowd—had now moved with deliberation to an area where there was no reason to go—no wagon, no outhouse, no picnic activity, no people. Just the thick, secret depths of the virgin bush.

Some impulse moved Linn toward the narrow passage through which Berry had just passed. Through the leafy sanctuary the pink dress glimmered, dappled by the shadows of the quivering poplar leaves.

Even as Linn watched, the slim figure was joined by another—lithely muscled, brown, vigorous—and her heart dropped and she felt as if she couldn't breathe.

As one hypnotized, Linn watched the dark head bend over the girl's lifted face, the strong, tanned arms close hungrily around her. Even to Linn's numbed senses there was passion evident in the embrace.

For the longest moment in her life she watched, turning the knife of another hurt, another humiliation, in her half-healed heart.

Then, as silently as she had come, she slipped away.

With unsteady legs and trembling hands, Linn went about packing her box and loading the wagon. That done, she went in search of her brother to tell him she was leaving.

Judd would stay, with Modesty, to join the group at the lake that evening. Stumbling back to collect her mother, Linn saw Trapp standing at the table, filling a cup with lemonade. He smiled, his dark eyes half shut against the brilliance of the sun. She passed him silently.

"Wait . . . ," he said, and her lips twisted at the naturalness of his tone.

"I'm going home."

"But I thought you were going to stay on."

"That was before. . . ." She couldn't say it over the pain in her throat.

"Before?"

"Oh, don't pretend!" she flashed.

Trapper Farley's eyebrows went up. "Would you mind explaining that?"

"Me—explain to you?" Linn laughed, but without humor.

Even to her own ears that laugh sounded reminiscent of her bitter outburst when Trapp had found her in the bush smarting over Abram's betrayal.

"Shouldn't I be the one to ask that of you?" she said now tightly. "But then, why should you give *me* an explanation? You don't owe me a thing. After all, what's one kiss?"

Trapper Farley's eyes narrowed, and still she pressed on, driven by a pain she had thought never to feel again. "A kiss in the bush. It seems a reasonable place for a woodsman to play at love, wouldn't you say?"

Into the well of silence that fell between them, pinning her there under that blue gaze, she added bitingly, "You operate well in the woods, Trapp!"

"Why are you saying these things?" Trapp said, standing close and holding her by the arms. "Why are you acting like this?"

"Oh, Trapp!" she said derisively, "you can stop the pretense! After all, I *saw* you!"

"You saw . . . ?"

"I saw! I followed Berry. Surely you don't think I'm such a simpleton that I didn't suspect there was something between you and Berry all the time!"

"Yes, I thought you might," he admitted. "But—you *followed* Berry?"

"What if I did?" Linn cried defensively, her humiliation and hurt greater than her shame at having done so.

Trapp looked sick.

"I see it all," she said, tears near the surface. "Easy Linn—that's it, isn't it, Trapp?"

"If you say so." Trapper Farley's eyes, as he turned away, were unfathomable.

18

TO THE CHEERS OF THE BYSTANDERS, MARC SLID into home base. Wiping the dust from his pants, he turned to the small slope where Charity sat, leaning indolently against a small poplar and flopped down beside her.

Expecting her usual red-lipped smile and warm eyes, he was taken aback when Charity turned her face away.

"Hey, what's wrong?" he asked, plucking a stalk of graceful wild oats and tickling her bare arm with it.

Charity drew away her arm. And instead of the high-handed answer she ordinarily would have given when peeved, she got to her feet, brushed off her dress, and walked away.

Marc's face was thoughtful as he watched her stride, body stiff and head high, toward the tables and the crowd there. He was accustomed to Charity's changeable moods, but this one didn't fit somehow, and he was uneasy.

Leaping to his feet, he hurried after her. Catching her by the arm and swinging her around, he said, as gently as he could, "Cherry? I don't understand—"

Charity's lips twisted and she cried contemptuously, "Oh you understand, all right!"

"I really don't," he protested. "Unless it's your mother. . . ."

Marc's narrowed eyes studied Charity's flushed, rebellious face.

"That's it, isn't it?" Marc continued. "Surely she can't object to our meeting here . . . publicly like this."

Charity stared over his shoulder, chin high, eyes cold.

"Cherry, you heard what I told her. We both know we have no choice right now, but—"

"Well, *I* do!" Charity's voice was as hard as her eyes. "*I* have a choice. And I refuse to talk to a—a coward!"

Under her bitter lashing, Marc's hand fell away from her arm, and he stepped back as though she had struck him a physical blow.

She turned with a flounce; he watched her go from him, his dreams lying wounded in his spirit. He wondered if they could survive this.

She's too childish after all, he thought sadly. She never has seen it . . . she won't see it . . . maybe she can't see it.

"Marc!" It was Rhoda Mason.

Rhoda, Kate Weatherby's sister, had arrived in Wild-rose recently and would stay all summer and through the birth of Kate's and Abram's baby.

"Tell me," Rhoda said brightly, taking the sturdy young man's arm. "What do you do for fun here in the summer?"

Marc allowed the girl to draw him over to the tables where Brother Victor was gathering everyone to the feast. But his mind was set: no more involvement with girls the age of Charity and Rhoda! And though this young miss chattered and flirted a bit, Marc's dull heart could not respond.

As for Charity, she had disappeared. The church ladies, foreheads and upper lips beaded with the perspiration of their efforts, stood shoulder to shoulder behind the stretching tables, ready to help reaching hands, replace empty platters with full ones, fill glasses with lemonade, and wave off flies.

Brother Victor stepped onto a box, called for attention, and when the noise had abated blessed the food, not daring to say more as the hungry crowd pressed toward the tables.

At the "Amen" the line formed rapidly, and people with heaping plates found places among family or friends in which to eat, to chat, to rest.

The general hubbub and confusion were interrupted by the approach of a smart rig, bouncing across the meadow behind a high-stepping horse. It was, obviously, the new "Bike Gear Runabout," and the men watched with quickened interest. Several rose to their feet, and when the minister strode toward the rig, they followed, eyes fixed on the runabout.

While Gerald Victor reached a hand to the young man now jumping lightly to the ground and uttered a warm greeting, the others searched the rig curiously for the "more than a hundred little special features" pledged by the manufacturer to make a "handsomer, stronger, easier riding, lighter draft, more stylish, more lasting" rig. The axles were of "high arch naked steel" and were "swaged, top and bottom"; the spindles were guaranteed to be "self-oiling, dust and mud proof."

Painted in the "best possible manner" and upholstered in "heavy light Bedford cord" (heavier than whipcord) and with a full length velvet carpet, padded patent leather dash, and good storm apron, it was a sight to behold as it sat, a swan among ducks, amid the battered buggies and weary wagons of Wildrose.

"Good day, Mr. Fairchild!" the pastor was saying. "I see you found us."

"Yes, sir," the young man answered, pulling off his tweedy cap and slapping it against his tweedy leg to remove the dust of the country roads, "with hardly any trouble at all, thanks to your fine directions."

In the sunlight, the young man's thick mop of hair was the color of winter butter. The pale head lifted above the minister and most of the men standing there. The face was open and frank, with a high, ruddy color.

"Men," the preacher said genially, "this is Benjamin Fairchild."

Friendly hands were extended in welcome, and questions followed concerning the performance of the runabout and particularly about the puzzling fifth wheel. After studying how it was indeed "riveted and brazed" to the front axle, as the catalog had explained, they followed the newcomer and the minister to the table area and to their half-eaten dinner.

Here the young man's stalwart build and attractive face were studied by the young women of the group. About 19 years old he appeared to be, if that. But he was greeting people with friendliness and ease and would not be a stranger for long.

Kate Weatherby stood beside Elva Victor and Maggie Edwards, serving beans and potato salad to the elderly Runyon brothers. "Who is that?" she asked, for the eyes of all three were on the new arrival, while the old men's plates waited expectantly.

Maggie shrugged and returned to her duties. Harry's rheumy eyes lit, and Hubert smacked his lips with anticipation as baked beans were heaped on their tipping plates.

"A very nice-seeming young man," Elva Victor answered Kate's question, adding a drumstick to Hubert's already-loaded plate.

"You've met him?"

"He came to the house yesterday," the minister's wife explained. "He's looking for someone. He told us all about it. Seems he's been looking up and down the country, but without any luck. Brother Victor suggested he come to the picnic today, since most everyone would be here and ask if anyone knew the folks he's interested in finding."

"Strange . . . ," murmured Kate, squinting her eyes against the sun and studying the young man. "He seems vaguely familiar, don't you think?"

Elva Victor looked at the young fellow critically, while

Maggie waved a tea towel over the potato salad at the ever-present flies.

"I never saw him before yesterday," Mrs. Victor said. "I imagine he is a person of some means—that's quite a rig he's driving. Staying in hotels isn't cheap either. How many of us could afford that? He's come all the way from British Columbia."

"None," thought Kate, unless it was Maggie and John Edwards, and no one seemed to know the extent of their resources, although it was suspected they had more income than they derived from the homestead.

As the minister's wife spoke, Maggie ceased her towel flapping and looked earnestly at the young stranger. Surrounded by the friendly crowd, the fair head gleamed in the noon sun.

* * *

When the stylish equipage had first pulled into the parsonage yard, Rev. Victor had been sermonizing. Laying his notes aside, he had stepped out onto the porch, his wife following and his children gathering from various corners of the property.

"How do you do?" Brother Victor said, extending his hand to the young man stepping down from the runabout. "I'm Gerald Victor."

"Benjamin Fairchild, sir."

"What can I do for you, Mr. Fairchild?"

"Well, to start off, call me Ben!" The stranger grinned engagingly, and it was obvious he was little more than an overgrown boy.

"Ben. Won't you come in?"

"Well, sir," the fresh-faced young man said after he had met Mrs. Victor and the children and had seated himself in the front room of the log parsonage, "I'm in the area looking for someone, and I hope you might help me."

"Be glad to if I can," Gerald Victor responded readily to the open smile of the young fellow. "What's the name?"

"Johnson—a couple by the last name of Johnson."

"Sorry," Rev. Victor said promptly, "there are no Johnsons in Wildrose. I can tell you that right off."

"But perhaps you've heard of them." Ben Fairchild persisted. "Mr. and Mrs. Ed Johnson."

Gerald Victor shook his head and looked at his wife. Elva looked mystified.

Obviously disappointed, the young man seemed reluctant to give up.

"Listen, son," the minister said kindly, "if it's important, and I assume it is, come to our picnic tomorrow. Most everyone from Wildrose will be there, as well as visitors from Cloud and other neighboring districts. Perhaps someone will recognize the name—could save you a lot of running around."

Ben Fairchild's face had brightened at the suggestion. "That's a splendid idea!" he exclaimed. "Now, if you'll be so kind as to tell me where it will be held—"

* * *

Now the minister cleared his throat, placed one hand on the arm of the stranger who had alighted from the expensive runabout, and raised the other for attention. The crowd silenced its chatter and turned toward their spiritual leader and the young man at his side—tall, with one lock of fair, thick hair falling over his forehead to show the side of a curious cowlick, his teeth large and white in a mouth that was smiling in a particularly sweet manner—for a man—above a handsome, deeply cleft chin.

Some dim memory struggled for recognition in Kate Weatherby's mind as the minister spoke.

"Friends, this young man is in our midst today looking for someone." He cleared his throat and looked kindly at the newcomer at his side. "Someone who means a great deal to him. I thought you might recognize the name and be able to help him. Kindly respond if you can . . ."

"I wish he'd get on with it," Kate thought with a flash

of impatience and a tension she didn't fully understand. "After all, he's not making an announcement in church now!"

But Rev. Victor enjoyed an audience, no matter where he found it, and continued in a leisurely, gracious manner. "And so I hope you will give him your cooperation today. We'll let him eat first, though, and then many of you will want to talk to him in more detail about the person he's looking for."

The minister smiled at the ladies as they reached automatically for a plate and utensils.

"So please," he continued, "welcome to our midst Benjamin Fairchild, and consider whether or not you may know an Edward and Marguerite Johnson."

The spell cast by the preacher's oratorical introduction was shattered abruptly when a gasp erupted from the group of women behind the tables and Maggie Edwards fell in a faint at their feet.

Even as Maggie collapsed and as they all stood transfixed, Kate's startled gaze caught the look of anguish in John Edwards' face before he thrust the crowd aside and sprang to the side of the prostrate woman.

"Help me, Kate!" he said as he knelt beside Maggie, straightening the crumpled form that was usually so regally held and now lay so limp and still.

Kate snatched up a tea towel, dipped it in water, and dropped to her knees beside John. She pressed the wet cloth to the pale forehead—one of Maggie's finest features, over which sprang a curious cowlick of fair, gray-touched hair.

The watching people stirred helplessly. Gerald Victor called for order, described the heat as overpowering, and reported that the fallen woman was coming around nicely.

Benjamin Fairchild, bending close, clutched the minister's arm and asked, "What's wrong? *Who is that?*"

"One of our ladies. I'm sure the heat and the excitement of the day have just been too much for her."

"*Who is she?*" Ben jockeyed to see more of the fainting woman, now stirring in her husband's arms.

"Her name," Brother Victor said patiently, "is Maggie Edwards. And that's her husband there, holding her: John. John and Maggie Edwards," he finished thoughtfully.

"John Edwards! Edward Johnson!" The young man's eyes were wide in his startled face. "Of course!"

Ben's long legs carried him around the table and to the side of the woman whose eyes, so like his own, were fixed on his from her position in her kneeling husband's arms.

With a sound between a sob and a laugh, Benjamin Fairchild knelt at Maggie Edwards' side.

Raising her hand toward him, Maggie whispered, "Benjie!" And John, wet-eyed, relinquished her to the strong young arms that reached for her.

19

WITH THE DAMP TEA TOWEL DANGLING LIMPLY from her hand, Kate watched the reunion, a stunned expression on her face. Fallen into place at last: the small, sweet-faced child in the gold frame. The missing gold frame. The missing child.

Maggie's eyes, always beautiful in their quiet strength, were shining with tears. They ran down her cheeks, past her trembling mouth, onto her dress.

"Benjie . . . Ben . . . little Ben," she murmured and rocked the big body in an ecstasy of joy.

John and Benjamin helped Maggie to her feet. With his arm around her, the young man led his mother tenderly toward his rig, while John had a few words with the minister and with Kate—the young woman who had boarded with them and to whom Maggie had said, "John and I have no children." Then, untying his own horse and climbing into his buggy, John followed Ben and Maggie from the lakeside, across the meadow, and home.

"What's going on?" Gabriel Goss, the Edwards' hired man, approached Kate where she was gathering her things together, as well as Maggie's, and packing them in boxes.

"You didn't hear?" Kate's voice was sharp. In spite of the months she had been married and lived away from the ferret-faced man, she carried a revulsion for him still.

"No, I didn't hear," he mimicked. "I was . . . otherwise engaged. What happened?"

"Maggie fainted."

"So I guessed. But who was that she went off with? And why is everyone standing around looking like cows waiting to be milked?"

At this uncalled for, unsavory remark, Kate's mouth set grimly, and she made no response.

"I'll just have to ask Dolly Trimble," Gabriel Goss said lightly.

"Oh, all right," Kate gritted. "You'll find out as soon as you get home, anyway. That young man," she hissed in a semiwhisper, "happens to be Maggie's son." But she hadn't been quiet enough; Dolly's alert ears had heard.

The look on that woman's face was a mix of consternation, wonder, dismay, and delight. Delight won.

"I always knew there was something funny there," she pronounced triumphantly to no one in particular. Her voice turned to a screech: "Albin! Albin!"

Albin stepped from the crowd, to stem as best he could the tirade into which Dolly was launched. Finally, in exasperation, he commanded, "That's enough Get our things together. Where are the girls?"

Modesty and Harmony came quickly and quietly. Eventually Charity was located, sauntering from some distant part of the lake, and the Trimble family joined the exodus.

Kate gave Gabriel Goss the box of things Maggie had left behind. "You know," she said to Abram, now standing at her shoulder, "I still can't abide that man. And you," she warned, turning to her young sister, "keep away from him!"

"Don't worry," Rhoda answered promptly. "But that new young man—who is he, did you say?"

"Yes, what's the story, Katy?" Abram asked. "Is that really John's and Maggie's son?"

"I don't know, but I don't think he's—John's." Kate bit her lip. "John just said 'Ben is Maggie's son,' and he asked me to take care of Maggie's things."

Abram scratched his head. "Whew! Talk about surprises! Maggie—with a grown son, a stranger! And John not the father?"

"I don't know," Kate said again, this time with a slight edge to her voice. "I'm sure we'll all find out in time." And she cast a glance toward the muttering Dolly. "Now, can we go home?"

What had been secret was secret no longer: John Edwards was the Edward Johnson the young stranger had been searching for. John explained the situation fully and soberly to Brother Victor and cared little how the story spread from there.

And spread it did, although, to give the minister credit, it wasn't due to indiscretion on his part. Like a prairie fire the story leaped from homestead to homestead until the district was caught up in the most excitement since Bruno Hilgen had turned a pail of chokecherries onto his wife's head, thus ceasing her endless grumblings—for the moment. "Perfectly good waste of chokecherries," was the general comment, or "Too bad she didn't swaller 'em—that woulda hushed her up!"

The "chokecherry cure" was recommended here and there for Dolly Trimble. Adept at twisting Scripture to her own advantage and with a store of remote passages on the tip of her tongue, Dolly now quoted, with satisfaction, "Some men's sins are open beforehand, going before to judgment; and some men they follow after."

"You should have a talk with Dolly," Elva Victor said worriedly to her husband. "She's on a rampage!"

"She'll be over—never doubt it," Dolly's concerned pastor said with a sigh, seeking a place of prayer to prepare himself for the counseling session that was certain to come.

* * *

Maggie's only explanation was made to Kate. "Do you remember the Peiping Pipeline?" Maggie had begun, adding, "You would have been very small. It was about 12 years ago."

"I've heard the term. I can't say I can recall the story."

"It was very big news at the time," Maggie said bitterly. "'Peiping Pipeline' was the term the newspaper picked up and used. It was a tremendous scandal, especially on the west coast. I had hoped never to hear the term again. For months there were reporters . . . port authorities . . . dreadful, dreadful to go through, a nightmare to remember."

Maggie's (Marguerite's) first husband and his brother had been importers of oriental art and rare porcelains. "At one time, I had a houseful of delicately carved ivory, cloisonné enamel, silks, and brocades sought by collectors everywhere—all very expensive, beautiful, and exceptional. And I accepted them as I accepted the bread and butter on my table, never questioning. I knew nothing of my husband's business then—and very little more now."

The Fairchild Brothers Import Export business had eventually come under scrutiny and was exposed as dealing in forbidden contraband, but even worse—Maggie now confessed with shamed face—illegal opium distribution.

When the scandal broke, the Fairchild men had hastily salvaged what they could and fled the country.

"They took with them," Maggie said in a choked voice, "my little boy. Damien, my husband, was devoted to Ben, as I was. I came home one day to find the house in confusion and Damien and Benjie gone, just gone.

"The manhunt was on, not only in Canada but also in the United States and eventually South America, to no avail. They never turned up one trace of them.

"I was under terrible suspicion," Maggie said. "The

police couldn't believe I didn't know about the cache of illicit goods in our warehouse, some of it displayed in plain view in my home.

"That's where John comes in—that's what I've called him for years now, rather than Edward. John is a lawyer, Kate."

Answered at last were the faint but persistent questions concerning John's qualities, his fine characteristics.

"He was the best. And I needed the best. It was a long, drawn-out affair, but in the end there was no proof that I had anything to do with any of the business."

Maggie went on to explain that, even after all the questions were settled about her involvement, there was no word of the missing men and the boy. For months it was rarely out of the public's mind, and Maggie was subjected to unrelenting surveillance. "It nearly drove me mad," she said.

"I seem to remember something about it," Kate said slowly. "Wasn't one of them found?"

"And not too far away, after all. It was Damien. He was sick—so sick he took the chance and went to a doctor in the Seattle area.

"Damien died. His family claimed his body and tried to have a private burial. It was chaotic. I felt torn limb from limb by the crowd—they were yelling, asking questions . . ."

"And Ben?"

"I suppose Damien had given Regis, his brother, instructions about Ben. They were gone. I've always felt that Damien's parents kept in touch with Ben somehow. As for me, I never heard one word."

Eventually, Maggie went on to explain, she had fallen in love with John. Their love, fresh and beautiful, was too precious to be blazoned across the world in headlines.

"John's uncle had homesteaded here—built the house and barn, cleared the land, and then became ill and returned to the coast. He offered it to John."

John, Maggie said softly, had left his business and his future and had brought her here to the "backwoods" and a new life.

The change of name? Simple protection. "The case was known everywhere. If I was ever to escape the suspicions, the questions, I had to start over.

"We have kept in touch with John's family," Maggie said, "but until three days ago, I was as separated from my child as if he had died."

The answer, pure and simple, was that Benjamin, as he grew up, remembered. Remembered enough to ask questions, to insist on answers, to be brave enough to make his way back to Vancouver and to the grandparents who had, indeed, kept in touch.

"They have had him in a good school and have been training him in the family business—they are also in the import business, but above reproach. Eventually, he was old enough to strike out on his own to look for me. In his persistence, he unearthed the record of my marriage to John and the clue about John's uncle's homestead in the bush country. The rest you know."

Kate's hand went out to clasp her friend's "What a terrible thing to happen to a mother!"

"It hasn't all been bad," Maggie said through her tears. "I've had John."

"And now you have Ben. What does the future hold for you, Maggie—you, John, and Ben?"

"John and I will stay in Wildrose," Maggie said, and Kate felt a surge of pride in her friend. Obviously she wasn't going to run again. "We may go back and see family and take care of some business there, but we'll come back—home."

"The Wildrose people, Maggie," Kate said with concern. "How are they going to take this? You know them better than I do."

"Yes, I know them, and I guess all of them are

stunned, some are even dismayed. Some, like Dolly Trimble, will be outraged. And believe me, Kate, I've felt guilty
about the deception. I wanted a new start, away from the
scandal, and now, well, now it seems to have followed me,
and it has all come out. I'll live with it."

Kate hugged her friend, determined to see it through
with her.

* * *

Dolly Trimble was indeed outraged—outraged and
vocal about it.

Dolly put on her hat and made a call on the preacher.

"What are you going to do about this situation?" she
demanded when she had deposited her rigid bulk in a
chair in the room the minister called his study.

"What *should* I do, Sister Trimble?"

"Why," spluttered Dolly, "they should be taken to
task! Living a lie . . . right in our midst! Scandalous!"

"Perhaps it should be considered their own business."

"Poppycock!" This was as near as Dolly came to
swearing. But her intent was the same. "It's your duty to
tackle sin and deception when it rears its ugly head, sir!"

"They are not children to be chastened, Sister Trimble,
at least not by me." Brother Victor's comment indicated he
realized they might well receive chastening from a Higher
Power.

"My responsibility, and yours, is to obey our Lord's
command, 'Judge not, and ye shall not be judged: con-
demn not, and ye shall not be condemned: forgive, and ye
shall be forgiven.'" The earnest voice had a plea for understanding in it.

But Dolly was inflexible. And she was not ignorant of
the Word, especially that which suited her need.

"Don't forget," she said triumphantly, "where it says
every tree is known by its fruit . . . a corrupt tree cannot
bring forth good fruit. It is to be hewn down and cast into
the fire, trodden under foot of man, cast into outer dark-

ness. . . ." In her vehemence, Dolly was mixing her quotations grotesquely. The minister might have laughed if it had not been so pathetic.

"Try to keep this in perspective, Sister Trimble," he said gently. "John and Maggie Edwards—"

"Edward and Marguerite Johnson!"

"—have made their peace with each other over this, with Ben, and, I trust, with God. Now they need to have peace with *us*, their Wildrose friends and neighbors."

"Peace? How can you say 'Peace, peace,' when there is no peace?" Dolly spouted, skilled at mangling the Word to suit her purposes. "Think of it! Charity has been in *that woman's* class!"

So it had come to *that woman*. The pastor sighed, "Maggie has resigned her class. And our youth will be much poorer because of it."

"Brother Victor!" Scandalized, Dolly Trimble summed up her opinion of "that woman": "Whited sepulchre! Tares in the midst of the wheat! Well, I can tell you this—as long as that woman so much as attends, I'll never darken the door of the church again!"

The minister was speechless before the onslaught. It would have helped if he had understood that Dolly, already secretly jealous of her neighbor, had found an outlet. Like a seething volcano, Dolly had virtually blown her top.

With her departure, Gerald Victor put his head down on the table that served as his desk and prayed: *O Lord— help me! Help me to help Dolly!*

When he raised his head, his eyes were lit with purpose. Without further ado, he shrugged himself into his coat, put his hat onto his head, strode to the kitchen, and announced to his wife, "I'm going to see Hubert and Harry. I need some powerful prayer support."

"From those old rapscallions?"

"Those *redeemed* old rapscallions. I'm beginning to think God has left them here in order to use them as prayer warriors. And do you know what? I think Hubert and Harry are beginning to believe it too."

"Who'd have thought it?" marveled the pastor's wife. "Hubert and Harry, unlearned in so many ways, mostly housebound, in frail health—strengthening the weak hands and confirming the feeble knees of those who are of a fearful heart."

"Like me," admitted the sorely tried pastor.

 **20**

THE FICKLE SUN CHANGED ITS MIND AGAIN. IT came early, stayed late, and glowed in the sky all day like a million and more parlor lamps, each ablaze with 85-candlepower strength.

Birds muted their silvery voice and sought midday shelter in the bush. Sloughs shriveled, and the rich grasses at their edges browned and drooped. Roads, always so mucky after a rain, dried into deep ruts and leveled out into sandy trails.

That tiny scourge of the north, the mosquito, followed the sun to summer and, with its usual exuberance and tenacity, plagued all flesh. Men built smudges, and stock, with twitching, insect-covered hides, made for the leafy shelter of the trees.

Sunsets transcended all others, or so the bush people believed, crowning their days with a glory only felt and rarely put into words. Many an impoverished farmer, lacking all but the barest necessities of life—and those in poor quality—felt himself blessed and enriched by skies as lovely as any painting in a king's royal gallery.

But as often as not, an awe-filled contemplation of the majestic sky would be rudely broken by the loon's laugh, echoing crazily across the water of the lakes, plummeting heavenly fantasy to harsh reality.

Farmers watched the thickening heads of grain with apprehension. Had planting been too late to allow for full maturing? Would summer depart abruptly and take with it their brief growing season? It was the time for waiting and for praying.

Gardens peaked, and berries in their turn hung ripe and full in the bush. When the canning and picking were done and the sealers and produce were taken to the cellar in a rite as old as housekeeping itself, winter's gathering shadow receded a little.

There were Sundays in Wildrose when every woman's hands were a peculiar shade of rose or blue in accordance with the fresh jars on her cellar shelves.

If parents worked from dawn to dark, children were in their element as winter-bleached faces and arms and legs became brown and soles of tender feet toughened. Bush children were as free-spirited as the birds that filled their days with song, and as happy as youngsters can be who are well-fed, sufficiently clothed, surrounded by families and friends, loved and disciplined, and who little know or understand the burdens and anxieties of those who make these blessings possible.

It was the proper time for the preacher's admonition "Remember now thy Creator in the days of thy youth, while the evil days come not, nor the years draw nigh, when thou shalt say, I have no pleasure in them."

Those who needed it most heeded it least and squirmed in their seats, waiting for release to the glorious summer that was slipping from them far too quickly.

Those who knew full well how rapidly the "silver cord" could be loosed, the "pitcher be broken at the fountain," and "the wheel broken at the cistern," sighed and mouthed the scripture's familiar conclusion: "Vanity of vanities, saith the preacher; all is vanity."

Linn drooped through the summer. Celia wondered and worried and prayed. There had been a certain sadness about her daughter since the picnic, and Celia suspected it had something to do with Trapper Farley.

When Trapp passed through their yard, Linn turned away or busied herself in some way. If they met, they exchanged brief nods.

Linn was sure Trapp often used the alternate road to his place, a much longer route, but one that avoided a meeting with her. Whether this was for his sake or hers she wasn't sure.

Perhaps most significant of all was the change in Berry Lille. Usually reserved, quiet, and restrained, she looked now as if an inner light had been turned on. Berry glowed. Everyone noticed it, Linn most of all.

Love had come in the summer to Wildrose and left its mark on one face, at least. That it left another full of misery was not totally unnoticed.

Picking wild strawberries one still, warm day, Linn came across Berry and stared in grudging admiration at the graceful form kneeling among the wild vines, her mouth touched with the scarlet juice, her skin a dusky apricot, her dark hair shining in the sun.

Berry looked up and smiled. Holding up a small, sweet strawberry, the young métis confided, "I made shortcake this morning."

Linn knew who would enjoy it for supper. "I'm going to make jam," she explained lamely and probably unnecessarily to Berry.

Berry dropped a handful of crimson jewels into her pail, and Linn wondered if, come winter, Berry's lovely face would sit across the breakfast table from Trapper Farley, lighting up for love of him while serving him strawberry jam. Shutting her eyes to the picture, she said, "Berry . . . I'm very happy for you."

Startled, Berry gave a low laugh. "Is it so plain? We have been trying to keep it a secret."

Catching her breath at this confirmation of her suspicions, Linn accidentally overturned her pail. Both girls scrambled to pick up the scattered fruit.

"We thought," Berry continued, "that no one knew . . ."

Linn made no response, but bent her face over the mat of vines, searching blindly among the leaves, and Berry said, gently, "Linn, perhaps I shouldn't say it, but I've sometimes thought maybe you . . . and Trapp . . ."

"No!" Linn said quickly. "Please believe me, Berry— truly, there's nothing between Trapp and me!"

"Sometimes I have this feeling that maybe you—" Berry hesitated, and again Linn spoke sharply, "What? I *what?*"

"Well, you don't seem your usual . . . happy self."

"I'm perfectly happy! Why shouldn't I be?"

Berry looked only half convinced, and Linn forced herself to further, safer, conversation. "I suppose you're making plans for the wedding."

"In a way," Berry said, returning stubbornly to her train of thought. "But I wanted to be sure, first, about you and Trapp. It would make a difference."

Noting Linn's set mouth, Berry sighed and said, "Well, there *are* things that have to be worked out. There's the matter of the house, for one thing. It's too small, of course, for three people. And naturally," Berry's voice turned shy, "we'd like to be alone if we can."

"Naturally."

"So either Trapp or Boyd will have to move out. They're discussing it, thinking about going their separate ways, one keeping the Cooley place and the other leaving. But I'm not sure I want to leave Wildrose, and I know Trapp doesn't."

"I can see that's something to work out," Linn murmured, her fingers busy in the grass, her head bent. Trapper Farley, she remembered desolately, was beginning to love Wildrose.

"There—I think that's all of them," Linn said briskly,

and made her escape, trusting she had carried the situation off well.

If she had looked back, she would have seen Berry watching her with troubled eyes.

21

DON'T FORGET—WE'RE GOING TO DO THE BEANS today!" Dolly warned her daughters at the breakfast table.

Modesty looked resigned, a disconsolate expression settled over the childish features of Harmony—she knew she would have to help pick and snap—and Charity stared wordlessly out the window.

Dolly continued, "And we'd better hop to it; it's going to be a real scorcher."

And a scorcher it was. When at last the jars were dropped into the hot-water bath, the kitchen was as hot as the garden patch. Only when the fruit of their combined efforts was cooling on the tabletop did a sort of grim satisfaction replace the short tempers of the grim workers.

While the last batch bubbled, the family gathered for the noon meal. Charity picked at the mix of potatoes and onions fried together and started when the screen door rattled to a loud knock.

Gabriel Goss stepped inside when Harmony opened the door.

"Brought your mail," he said placidly and laid a few papers on the table.

"Why, thanks, Gabe," Albin said heartily. "We haven't been to town in a month of Sundays. Probably won't get there soon, either."

Gabriel Goss didn't seem inclined to linger. Bowing to the ladies in a manner uncharacteristic of bush people, he said, "Mrs. Trimble . . . Modesty . . . Harmony . . . Charity." And turning, he clumped in heavy work boots toward the door.

"Well, I never!" Dolly spluttered. "What do you make of that?"

"Neighbors often bring mail by," Albin reminded her.

"Yes, but not him. And especially since that shameful development at the Edwards'—Johnson's—place. If they think they can be accepted by decent people just like that, they've got another think coming!"

Albin sighed, "Now, Mother—"

"Don't you 'Mother' me, Albin Trimble! Surely you know how shocked I am about the—the scandal over there!"

"I know, all right," Albin admitted and subsided, hoping for peace.

But Dolly wasn't finished. "If they think they can wipe out their lies by delivering a few papers . . ." Her face was flushed with far more than the heat of the stove over which she had been bending. "After all—sin's sin, and it can't be condoned!"

Albin pushed back his chair; his face showed his dismay. His wife's zealous denunciation of sin included the sinner. "Dolly . . . Dolly . . . ," he murmured, shaking his head.

On his way out of the room, Albin stopped at his wife's side and touched her heaving shoulder. "Whatever happened to 'love thy neighbour as thyself'?" he asked.

Dolly's mouth dropped open, and her face, if possible, became even redder than sun and stove had made it. "Al—"

"I'm going out," Charity interrupted abruptly. Turning to her sister, she asked, "Will you take care of the dishes this time, Moddy?"

"Sure, Sis."

Charity's decision was not an unusual one. She had spent a great deal of time away from the house all summer. Modesty understood her sister's restlessness and sympathized. She knew her well and was beginning to feel that all was not well somehow. Pondering the problem, she cleared the table, washed the dishes, and sprinkled down some ironing to be done when the day cooled.

Finally, weary and troubled, she took off her pinafore, rinsed her hot face, and turned to the room she and Charity had shared since babyhood.

Standing in the middle of the small space, a sudden chill touched Modesty's heart. Something—something was wrong.

A slight difference in the room's arrangement caught her attention: Charity's shoes—her Sunday shoes—were gone.

For the space of a heartbeat Modesty was puzzled. Then comprehension, like a small explosion, burst upon her. Swiftly she pulled out Charity's dresser drawer—and stood looking numbly at the few garments tumbled there.

Beyond the door she could hear her mother's voice and the slam of the screen door as Harmony went outside. Silence reigned, and still Modesty stood motionless with the evidence of her sister's absence.

But she was not in a daze; her mind worked swiftly. That Charity had slipped away she knew. But where had she gone?

Perhaps some dim hope that Charity would return caused Modesty to close the drawer quietly and return to the kitchen. But more likely there was a faint echo of applause in her heart for her sister's bold bid for independence.

Dolly was ready to remove the last batch of jars from the great kettle, and if her oldest daughter's face was touched with a trace of shock, it passed unnoticed.

As the afternoon waned, Dolly grew provoked with

Charity's absence. But she was often provoked with this middle daughter. And if truth were told, she was provoked with herself.

There were times when Dolly wished heartily that she had never gotten herself into this particular predicament. If only it were easier to admit a mistake. Or if only Albin had exercised his God-given authority and forbidden her to lay down the law so adamantly.

But in her most honest moments, Dolly knew she had insisted on having her own way, and she determined to see it through, hoping for the best.

When the cows came home by themselves in the late afternoon, ambling up the lane to stand lowing at the gate, it was suddenly clear that something was amiss.

"Albin," Dolly called, "did Charity bring the cows in?"

Albin's shouted "No!" alarmed her, and she hurried to the barnyard to check. There was no sign of Charity.

Dolly turned quickly, in spite of her bulk, and with Albin at her heels hurried toward the house. She slammed open the screen door and passed a startled Harmony and a watchful Modesty, strode through the house, and flung open the bedroom door. Her eyes ran over the empty pegs on the wall, and she yanked open the dresser drawer. One glance confirmed her suspicions.

"She's gone," she said flatly, as she turned to face the three people in the doorway.

Herding them into the front room, Dolly seated them and made plans. "Nothing has happened to her—that we know," she said grimly. "She hasn't been abducted, she isn't lying injured in the fields or meadow, and she isn't asleep somewhere. She's gone, and of her own accord. This means there's no need to tell the police or organize a search. She left deliberately."

Albin frowned sharply, and she cried, "Albin! Let me have my way in this! Surely you know what this means to me!"

And Albin, knowing, let her.

"It won't be for long. We'll find her."

When Modesty looked doubtful, Dolly added, "Well, where in the world could she go?"

Modesty could only shake her head helplessly, having already gone over that and coming up with no answers.

"The only possible place is to your sister's, Albin."

It seemed reasonable. Where, on the meager amount of money she had—a couple of dollars hoarded from egg money from her own banty hens—could Charity go?

"I'll go to P.A. first thing tomorrow," Albin said, "and bring her home." After a moment's reflection he added, "If she'll come."

"Of course, she'll come! She's your child, isn't she? If you're in doubt, I'll go myself!"

"I'll go," Albin said firmly, and Dolly subsided.

With due warning to Harmony to "keep quiet about this," the evening routine was resumed. But a certain dismay had touched all of them, and an uneasiness hovered over the supper table.

O Lord, Modesty prayed that night, lying in bed without her sister for the first time in memory, *please look after Charity!* Half-sympathetic with her sister's unhappy state, she couldn't bring herself to ask, "Bring her back."

It was an omission she was to regret.

The three of them—Dolly, Modesty, Harmony—went about the activities of the following day as normally as possible. Dolly staunchly maintained that Charity would be back with her father. Modesty was touched when her mother made a batch of butter tarts, Charity's favorite.

When Albin drove in late in the day, alone, Dolly's face whitened.

"She's not with Hilda," Albin said, creaking stiffly from the buggy to face the three remaining females of his family. "Hilda hasn't seen her or heard from her."

"Then she's with Marc—Marc Szarvas," Dolly said, as

if the thought had been on the horizon of her mind. And in spite of her oft-stated objections to that young man, relief touched her face.

"No," Albin said, "I saw the Szarvas family coming back from a trip to town. Marc was with them, but not Charity."

Dolly crumpled. "Oh, Albin! Where's my baby?"

Two desperate days went by. Albin went doggedly about his work. Dolly tried to do the same, but it was clear her heart was gripped by an anxiety bordering on frenzy. Charity would—she *must*—contact her family soon!

But where was she? Whom was she with? What was she doing? Dolly's overactive imagination conjured up answers that served only to inflame her fears. At times she came near crying out, "Oh, if only I'd been less severe!" But it was not a weakness she admitted aloud.

Sunday came, and Dolly insisted that Modesty must attend church. "We have to carry on as usual," she said, hoping the week would bring Charity back and the problem to an end quietly and decently. "No one will wonder why I'm not there, not with Maggie Edwards attending just as if nothing had happened." Catching her husband's pained glance, Dolly dropped the subject.

So Modesty went. And true, everyone seemed to realize why Dolly wasn't there, and since Charity hadn't been faithful in attendance since Maggie had resigned as teacher of her class, her absence also went unremarked.

Judd Graham walked Modesty home when church was dismissed. In his caring presence a tear slipped over Modesty's lashes, and with a sob the story came out.

Judd pressed the small hand in his and looked thoughtful. "Something occurred to me while you were talking," he said. "Did you know Gabriel Goss is gone?"

Modesty stopped in the dusty road, her eyes on Judd's face. "What are you saying?"

"I'm just wondering, is all. Gabe quit his place at the Edwardses and left Wildrose on Thursday."

"Thursday! That's the same day . . ."

"Can it be a coincidence? How could Charity get away without help? She didn't take a horse, she didn't have any money to speak of, and she took her things. It looks as if it was planned."

Modesty moaned. "Oh, no . . . no. This is terrible! How can I tell Mum?"

"Perhaps you shouldn't—I don't know. You'll just have to think about it. After all, we're not sure." And Judd turned back, leaving Modesty to make her reluctant way homeward.

Before the day was over, Modesty had come to the conclusion that she would have to speak out. Her mother wasn't eating, and she had a feverish look about her; her eyes had a haunted expression. If Gabriel Goss's leaving Wildrose was a clue that would lead to Charity, it would be worth the initial anguish it would cause.

Nevertheless, Modesty approached her parents hesitantly. "I heard something this morning . . . maybe I should mention it?"

Two pairs of eyes looked at her hopefully.

"It may not mean anything . . ."

Impatience flashed in Dolly's eyes, and Albin said gently, "Speak up, Moddy."

"Well, Gabriel Goss . . ."

"Gabriel Goss *what*?"

Modesty moistened dry lips. "He's—he's quit his job. He left Wildrose."

Dolly frowned, slow wheels turning. Albin looked fixedly at his daughter. It was he who asked, "When?"

"Thursday."

Dolly sat down abruptly, all the color draining from her face. Albin took his wife's limp hand in his and rubbed it soothingly.

"Try and keep calm, Mother," he said as firmly as he could before her stricken face. "There may be no connection."

"How did he go?" Dolly asked in a muffled voice.

"I don't know. We could ask the Edwardses, I suppose."

"Never!" Dolly's voice took on a hysterical tone.

"By train, no doubt," Albin said thoughtfully.

"Albin," Dolly cried, "go to the station. Talk with Rudy."

Without a word, Albin made preparations to go to Meridian. The three hours of his absence seemed like an eternity to the waiting women. He returned with news both bad and good.

"Well," he said heavily, "she left Meridian Thursday—with Gabriel Goss."

Dolly was stony-faced. Modesty began to cry.

"Rudy says Gabe bought two tickets. Although Charity didn't go into the station house, he saw her plain enough. They got on the train together. The tickets were for Moose Jaw."

Dolly well knew Rudy's curiosity. His glance would be sharp, and he had known Charity since she was born. There was no questioning his story.

"So then—everybody knows," Dolly said faintly.

"Or will," agreed Albin.

Albin got to his feet, straightened his rawboned frame, and said, "We're going to quit this ridiculous pretense, Dolly."

In response to his wife's tearful look, he added firmly, "It was all right, I guess, when there was a chance Charity might get home without anyone knowing. For her sake I kept quiet and prayed for the best. All along—through this thing about Marc, and then Maggie and John, and now this—I've let you assume a holier-than-thou attitude, which is just plain silly, if not downright . . . sinful!"

Dolly blanched at the word.

"You might think over your attitude toward our neighbors, who've always been good ones," Albin said. "Your criticism of them—in light of what we have here—seems pretty pointless, I'd say."

All the fight was gone from Dolly. As always, she knew when Albin had reached the end of his patience. Oh, if only he hadn't been so long in coming to it! There was security in turning things over to him, much as she struggled to keep from doing it.

Dolly's head dropped onto her arms on the tabletop. Albin put his hand on her bowed head, and said, "I'll go and talk with Brother Victor. Then we'll carry on as best we can. We'll hear where Charity is eventually and then we'll know what to do next."

22

S PRING'S DELICATE FRAGRANCE HAD BUR-
geoned into the pungent aromas of summer. Now a
slow decay was setting in. It was marked by a certain pi-
quant odor—not unpleasant, but different—of grasses
withered, berries shriveling in the heat, hay drying in the
meadows, and grain maturing on the stalk.

Farmers watched the sky anxiously, rubbing heads of
wheat in calloused hands, blowing chaff, and shaking their
heads over grain that threatened to be stunted in size and
poor in quality. Most of their livelihood lay spread out before them in a few acres of land wrenched from the bush
not too many years previous and tussled with ever since in
an effort to force from it a foreign kind of crop.

Winter's shadow crept insidiously over the hills from
the north. For the industrious, it was a busy time.

And Wildrose people were industrious, by necessity, if
not by nature. They felt the Bible should include—or did
it?—the maxim "God helps those who help themselves."
Like the squirrel that instinctively forages and stores food
for winter, the people of the bush felt an urgency to pro-
vide for the inevitable hibernation that was to come.

But even the industrious and the diligent are subject to
the whims of nature, and there were those years when
crops failed, hens were off their laying, and cows dried up
too soon.

They lived on the precipice of disaster. The consoling feature was that what happened to one usually happened to all. They stood or they fell together. They enjoyed a measure of bounty, bowed heads and thanked God together, or tightened their belts and made do, bowed their knees, and besought God together.

Judd Graham had been tense and anxious, awaiting his turn with the threshing machine, fearful the weather would turn bad. He had been helping his neighbors, and they in turn were to follow the equipment to his place.

After an exhausting day at the Farley farm, Judd dragged himself home to bathe in the tub of tepid water waiting in the middle of the kitchen floor. All around were signs of the preparations Mum and Linn had made for the following day; the crew would arrive at sunup.

Fresh bread, covered with a white cloth, cooled on the table, pies dripped juice in the warming oven, and a freshly iced cake rested in the cupboard. The table in the other room was open full-length, covered, and set for the first of the three big meals to be served to the hungry threshers.

Preparing for threshing day, Linn had come to a conclusion: When harvest was completed, she would make a new life for herself, probably in Prince Albert. Perhaps in time Mum would join her, leaving the small house for Judd and Modesty; they couldn't make serious plans otherwise.

But the motivating reason was really Trapper Farley. Linn wanted desperately to get away from his presence—and the contented face of Berry Lille.

Linn's foolish expectations where Abram Weatherby was concerned had been painful; she still burned with humiliation and anguish when she thought about it—humiliation because she had been naive enough to take Abram's attentions seriously; anguish because he had so easily shrugged her from his thoughts.

But now, all that seemed inconsequential in the light of the later feeling that had trembled in her heart for Trapper Farley. Here, she had thought, was a real man, a man of scruples, a man of principles. Yes, she added, with a bitter thought, a man of *Christian* principles. Trusting a second time, her heart had opened like—like a wild crocus to spring sunshine.

To have been so wrong—again! To be so betrayed—again! She would get out now, although she knew Trapp would be moving soon, and Berry with him. Good luck to Berry Lille!

Up before dawn, Linn had dressed with care and tied her vibrant hair out of the way. At the last moment she tore the ribbon off and thrust it back in the drawer, snatched off the dainty apron she had put on, and tied an old pinafore—clean but faded—around her middle.

When the first hayracks creaked into the yard, she retreated to the range, and when the men filed in, entering the low house through the kitchen door behind her and passing into the only other room the ground floor boasted, she was bent over the frying pan. Never had eggs been so well-scrambled.

When the blessing had been said by Judd—stammering but committed to his spiritual responsibilities—Celia and Linn carried heaping platters of eggs, potatoes, sausages, pancakes, biscuits, and golden syrup, jams and jellics, great pots of tea and coffee, and pitchers of milk to be handed around and quickly emptied and refilled.

Linn kept her gaze from the end of the table where Trapper Farley was seated and retired to the kitchen as soon as possible. She was relieved when chairs and benches were shoved out of the way and the men trooped out to the fields.

After clearing the table, doing the mountain of dishes, and tidying the rooms, Celia and Linn started on the noon meal, "dinner" to bush people. Potatoes were peeled, corn shucked, cabbage cut and slaw made, chickens fried and johnnycake baked.

"Time to take out drinks and sandwiches, Linn," Celia reminded in the middle of the morning, and Linn lugged a basket toward the huffing, puffing engine and the men, like ants, scurrying around it. She was keenly aware of the tall figure atop a load of sheaves, and she felt awkward and hated it. If Trapper Farley saw her, she never knew. And not knowing, she was strangely disappointed.

Abram Weatherby, on the other hand, called a greeting to her and jumped down from his rick to help her with her load; was it possible his eyes rested on her with a touch of some forgotten meaning in them? A year ago, she thought, Abram's interest would have set her pulses racing and her hopes rising. Now she wondered about it, feeling uneasy and wishing he wouldn't.

Hot, thirsty, smelly, and dusty, the men came to the house at noon. At basins on a bench outside the door they washed, dunking dusty heads and shaking water everywhere.

Groping blindly for a towel, his black hair curly and shiny with sun and water, Trapper Farley's hand touched Linn's briefly. With a word of thanks, he bent his head and toweled vigorously.

"Well, what did you expect?" she scolded herself. Nevertheless, she was startled and shaken and turned away in a pain she had thought never to feel so sharply again.

During the meal and the one that followed late in the day, Trapp's gaze never lifted in Linn's direction; it seemed the proper behavior for a man engaged to be married, she thought wearily.

The bone-weary men shoved back from the supper table, stretched aching muscles, and made for their horses and rigs; they would be at the Szarvas homestead by sunup.

Celia was white-faced and exhausted. Linn shooed her mother upstairs and set about the task of bringing order out of chaos.

With a light rap on the screen door, Trapper Farley entered the house, stepping toward the lamplight and Linn.

"I forgot my hat," he explained.

A startled Linn stood in the ring of lamplight with his old hat in her hand; as if it burned her, she dropped it into his extended palm.

"Thanks," he said politely, and Linn turned from him abruptly.

Trapper Farley's voice, gentle, stopped her. "Lo, it was all grown over with thorns," he said.

Linn turned back, her eyes puzzled.

"Something a very wise man said a long time ago," Trapp said. "Actually he was talking about a field, overgrown with thistles and covered with nettles."

Jamming his shapeless old hat on his head and moving toward the door, he finished quietly: "Just for a moment there I thought I caught a glimpse of it . . . that lovely place made for spring crocuses and wild roses, choked by thistles and nettles."

And on these surprising words, Trapper Farley took his departure.

23

AS DOLLY HAD FEARED, THE NEWS SPREAD like wildfire. Rudy, the Meridian station master, lived up to his reputation.

He had thought it strange, Rudy clucked, when Gabriel Goss, the Edwardses' hired man, had bought two tickets. It had looked mighty bad to him, he said with a shake of his head, when young Charity Trimble from Wildrose seemed to be Goss's traveling companion. And he had been flabbergasted, he maintained, when he discovered their destination was not Prince Albert, a reasonable journey for a day of shopping, but Moose Jaw.

"Yessir," said Rudy, and more than once, "the minute he said, 'Gimmee two tickets to Moose Jaw,' I knew something was haywire! But natcherly, I didn't think anything was, er, *wrong*, if you know what I mean." And Rudy winked suggestively so that anyone listening immediately concluded that something was indeed very wrong. "Or else I'da talked to her, like as if she was my own daughter."

The accounts of Rudy's garrulousness seeped back to Dolly, shriveling her proud spirit. If gnashing teeth would have helped, Dolly would have indulged in it, so exercised was she with frustration and helplessness.

The humiliation was bad enough; worse by far was the realization that she was responsible.

Dolly was honest with herself at last. "If only . . . if on-ly . . . ," she kept crying, wringing her hands until Albin told her to stop condemning herself and spend her efforts in seeing how the situation could be remedied—or, he added with a meaningful glance toward little Harmony, how to keep it from happening again.

* * *

"Never have chickens so beautifully come home to roost!" crowed Kate.

But Maggie's generous heart was touched by Dolly's predicament. As Dolly loudly proclaimed the merits of righteousness and just as loudly denounced the poor person who fell short, she was caught in a web of her own weaving.

And Maggie was sincerely concerned for Charity. She had grown close to the girl, not only through years of Sunday School association, but through the more recent times when Charity had sought her out, haltingly and tentatively reaching for sympathy and understanding. Knowing Dolly well, Maggie had been cautious in her response. Now she, too, at times, reproached herself with "If only . . ."

"It does me good," Kate continued, "to see that woman get her comeuppance!"

Maggie shook her head. "I sympathize with Dolly," she said thoughtfully, "because for so many years I spent long nights wondering where Ben was . . . what he was do-ing . . . how he was being treated . . . who was looking after him when he was sick."

"But Ben was little, and he didn't make the choice that took him away from you."

"Yes, and that must make it all the more painful for Dolly. I'd like so very much to put my arms around her—"

"Better not try," Kate said with a shake of the head. "You'd probably get spit in your face for your trouble!"

"There must be some way. I think, Kate, we need a higher power to help us here."

And the two friends joined hands and, after some reluctance on Kate's part, hearts, breathing a prayer for the
shattered neighborly relationship.

* * *

Kate would not be returning to her position as teacher
of the Wildrose school.

By correspondence, the school board engaged a new
teacher. At almost the last hour a letter informed them of a
sudden illness and the woman's inability to keep the ap-
pointment.

The board was in a quandary; more meetings, more
waiting, more letters, all added up to a dim outlook for a
timely opening of school.

It was Gerald Victor who asked, "How about Maggie's
son, Ben Fairchild?"

"He's certainly qualified," John Edwards said, consid-
ering the idea.

"I'm all for it!" Albin Trimble said heartily.

"I can ask him," John said. "He wants to stay in Wildrose, at least for a while. Before winter's over, he may welcome something to do. He might just consider it."

Consider it he did, but not for long: "I'll do it!" was
his almost immediate decision. "At least I'll start the year
off for you. If someone else comes along, grab her when
you get the chance!"

"I'll be glad to help in any way I can," Kate promised.
"Remember—I started out green just a year ago, and if I
could tackle it, you certainly can."

* * *

When word of Charity's disappearance with Gabriel
Goss reached Marc, he left his parents' house and the concerned look on his mother's face, shut the door quietly behind him, and sought the seclusion of the barn.

There, in the dark and odorous privacy, he slammed
his fist violently against a wall and was unaware of the

pain to his body while the hurt in his throat swelled and swelled and threatened to choke him. With great, gulping breaths—a torn heart's way of sobbing when manhood forbids otherwise—he staggered around, ricocheting blindly from stall to stall until a semblance of reason returned.

There, in the noxious atmosphere, Marc wrenched his dreams from his heart and bitterly discarded his "schedule" in a purging as painful as the human heart can endure and yet survive.

The barn door closed, when Marc left, on wasted hopes as surely as if the brief moment of his spirit's groaning had expelled them from him.

Not far from the barn the wild rose hips flamed rusty red and orange, its dusky petals withered at its feet or blown to distant places, its last fragrances dispersed as surely as all sweetness had departed from Marc's life.

But unseen, as summer departed, she had scattered a store of seeds behind her; they held the life that made the bush country what it was. Given another spring, they would burst to new life, and the whirligig of seasons would spin again.

But for Marc, wounded and bereft and past caring, winter had set in, deep, silent, and cold in his heart.

24

LIFTING FROM GRATEFUL HEARTS, PRAISE RE-
sounded throughout the bush country: the crop was in.
And, for this year at least, it was a good one.

Hopes were high for refurbishing skimpy wardrobes
and obtaining items only dreamed of until now, even some
small luxuries.

And where better than through the "wish book" that
graced most prairie and bush homes with its gold mine of
goods?—"Something for everyone and quite a bit for
most."

You could order a pin or a piano, a button or a buggy,
a mousetrap or a roller organ and have it delivered to your
post office.

"Tell us what you want in your own way," the catalog
urged. "Write in any language, no matter whether good or
bad writing, and the goods will be promptly sent to you."
With such an invitation, what excuse was there for not or-
dering the desire of your heart?

Now was the chance to have, as your very own, a
Kant-Choke Nipple, Obesity Belt, Crow Caller, or the latest
hand-cut Jewel Hat Pin.

One's head whirled and one's choices faltered when it
came to milk skimmers, mincing knives, ball-pointed hair
wavers, wire fly killers, braided whip snappers, cold-han-

dle bent stove pokers, pocket match safes, oval foot tubs, thigh leggings and overgaiters, and wire hair rolls.

For sun-blistered faces and work-hardened hands, one could order Milk of Roses, Milk of Cucumber, Creme de Marshmallow, White Lily Face Wash. Eau de Quinine Hair Tonic promised luxuriant scalp stimulation. Beauty was about to blossom in Wildrose—in the winter.

With the nearest doctor miles away, Wildrose prepared itself for a healthy winter. For 15 cents (two cents extra for postage), 24 different Handy Pocket Tablet Remedies were available in "neat pleasant tablet form in small vest pocket glass bottles with metal screw top. THE EXPERIENCE OF MANY ABLE DOCTORS has been boiled down to produce in this compact form THE BEST KNOWN SCIENTIFIC TREATMENT FOR Nervous Trouble, Fever, Neuralgia, Pimples, Mumps, Croup, Alterative for the Blood, Kidney and Liver, Cold in the Head, Pleurisy, Dyspepsia, Colic . . ." and more was the guarantee. Good health was affordable!

For Marc Szarvas, finishing his small house in spite of dead dreams and dashed hopes, it was a bitter time.

"I'm going to finish it," he told his family as he built. "I'll move in by myself. I won't be the first man to batch."

His share of the crop money went for windows, stovepipes, and—his one-time dream—a Black Enameled Steel Range. When it sat in splendor in his lonely room, Marc cooked his lonely meals in an endless round of lonely days and lonelier nights.

* * *

In the Trimble household, even the purchase of a new cream separator could not lift the pall that existed due to Charity's unexplained absence. Day followed dreary day with no news.

Dolly—once proud, and vocally so—had been reduced not only in the community's eyes but in her own: righteousness had been revealed as self-righteousness.

When the false standard had been ripped aside, Dolly was left ashamed in the ugly revelation.

Always full-figured, Dolly lost weight alarmingly. Her eyes lost their spark and assumed a sick look as if the hurt on the inside was peering through the apertures.

Maggie, after prayer and filled with pity for her self-proclaimed enemy, offered to make the first move toward a reconciliation.

"Leave her be a while longer," her pastor advised. "There's an inner work going on, and we can't hurry it. With the good Lord's help, Dolly will come through it a better person."

When the letter arrived, it came to Brother Victor. And it wasn't from Charity.

The minister put on his coat and hat and walked from the parsonage to the Trimble homestead. Modesty answered his knock and invited him in.

"I'll call Mother," she said.

"Call your father too, Modesty. I need to see both of them."

Modesty seated the preacher, called her mother, and ran to locate her father. Then the three of them—Albin, Dolly, and Modesty—looked expectantly toward their pastor.

"I have here," Gerald Victor flourished the letter, "word from an associate of mine from the Moose Jaw circuit. It contains news of Charity."

Dolly's hands tightened convulsively. "At last," she breathed.

"Perhaps I should just read it. He—Brother Higgins—writes, 'A member of my church, a Mrs. Murdoch, has told me that she has hired a young woman from the Meridian area to work in her boardinghouse. Mrs. Murdoch says the girl is very young to be out working on her own but begged for the job. Also, the girl is not in good health, and she seems to be alone. Mrs. Murdoch wants to know if I can help locate the girl's family. I remember you from our conference, dear brother, and located your address in our minutes and have taken the liberty to write and ask if you know anything of this situation.'

"He goes on," Brother Victor added, "to name the girl as Charity and to say he'll help in any way he can."

"Charity! Working in a boardinghouse!"

"And all alone . . . I don't understand!"

"And sick!"

Consternation was written on the faces of the family.

Dolly turned to her husband. "What shall we do, Albin?"

"We'll go to her, of course."

"But . . . will she see us?"

"Would you like me to go?" Brother Victor asked.

Relief flooded the faces of Charity's parents. "I'll take you to the train, Brother Victor," Albin said promptly, "and buy the ticket. When can you go?"

"Tomorrow should be fine, Albin. Do you want me to bring Charity home?" It seemed a strange question, but obviously one he felt he should ask.

Dolly drew in her breath audibly, "Yes, Oh, yes."

"Tell her we want her to come home," Albin confirmed.

25

A S LIFE IN THE BUSH SLOWED DOWN IN PREPA-
ration of its long sleep following its burst of reproduc-
tion, the life cycle started among one of its species. A tenderly planted seed, lovingly nurtured, struggled forth to
lusty life.

As feared, old Doc didn't make it in time for the birth.
Abram had gone to get him, to find him far gone "in his
cups," and precious time was wasted in sobering the old
man. In so doing, Abram missed completely the chilling
and exhilarating drama of childbirth.

On his way to St. Clair and the doctor's residence,
Abram stopped at the Szarvas place, and Marte, herself the
mother of a brood of nine, of which Marc was fifth, went
immediately to be with her young neighbor at the birth of
her first child.

Though a novice at the job, Kate performed heroically.
Knowing how Marte had delivered some of her own children, with no fuss and little fanfare, Kate gritted her teeth,
submitted herself to Marte's instructions, and was shortly
delivered of a baby girl.

Eventually arriving, old Doc bumbled around and,
aware of Marte Szarvas's expertise, found little to do and
pronounced Kate in satisfactory condition and the baby
normal and healthy.

"And beautiful!" murmured an awed Abram, bending over the tender scrap of new life.

Marte offered to see that Doc got back to St. Clair, and they departed together.

"I'll be back each day for a while," Marte said in her heavily accented way, a concession to the fact that modern mothers were recognized to be more fragile than old-country women.

"Not that she wasn't brave," Marte reported to her family. "She did just fine—a good strong woman and a good strong baby. But she'll feel better if I go and tell her so."

The wee mite lay flannel-wrapped in her father's arms and the resemblance, even in those first hours, was remarkable.

"Just look, Abram—she's just like you!"

"You're right—she's the picture of Abram," agreed an adoring Aunt Rhoda.

The pink fingers curled around Abram's big thumb, to his amazement and pride. "I can see she's going to be her daddy's girl! Who needs a boy?"

Kate relaxed, having harbored a small fear that Abram might be disappointed because the first one was a girl. She took the babe, so lately torn from her own body, into her arms, touching the black curling hair, the silky cheek, the perfect hand.

"What shall we name her? . . . it has to be just right."

Kate moved the formless bundle to an upright position momentarily, and the dark head bobbed like a blossom on a frail stem. "Just like a rose . . . ," she crooned as she laid her cheek against the small one, so petal soft.

"Pearl!" Abram said suddenly, perhaps inspired by the matchless worth of this small gift.

"No, not Pearl. And not Ruby or Joy, or even Angela or Darlene. I've thought of those names, sweet though they are and descriptive of her in some ways. I think I know—"

Abram and Rhoda awaited expectantly.

"She's so like a rose, Abram."

"Rosy, Posy, pudding and pie . . ."

"Be serious, Abram! How about Rose? For our own flower, from our own seed." Kate blushed a little, glancing at her sister, who tried to look impassive.

"You know I love the wild rose," Kate continued. "It seems so . . . sort of significant, blooming as it does after the hard season is past."

"Rose," Abram savored the sound. "Rose . . . bud. That's what she is right now."

"I think she'll be Rosebud for now. And when she's older, Rose . . . Budd . . . whatever she chooses."

"Our own flower garden!" Abram said. "Soon there'll be Daisy and Violet and Marigold and Geranium and . . ."

"But wild roses," Kate said, tiredly and happily closing her eyes, "are the sweetest."

 **26**

THE TRIMBLE HOUSEHOLD WAITED TENSELY FOR their pastor's return. Dolly, pacing the floor, wondered if things could ever be the same again; Modesty, in a flurry of cleaning and baking, was certain they could not.

When Gerald Victor was seated again in the Trimble home, with the shadows of the autumn sun drifting through the lace curtains to vie with the floral pattern of the linoleum on the floor, three pairs of worried eyes studied his face.

"Brother Higgins took me to his home," he began. "Soon, as arranged, Mrs. Murdoch arrived, and we had a talk."

"Charity didn't come with her?"

"Mrs. Murdoch said Charity would come talk to me that evening. But when the time came, it was Mrs. Murdoch only. Charity refused to talk to me."

Dolly wilted. "Refused—?"

"Yes, absolutely. Nothing I could say, through Mrs. Murdoch, could persuade her. And Mrs. Murdoch—a real friend to Charity, by the way—wouldn't agree to my going to her place without Charity's permission."

"What more did this Mrs. Murdoch have to say?" asked Dolly anxiously.

"She said Charity is doing a good job and that she is a

fine worker. She seems to be genuinely fond of her." Brother Victor hesitated. "But, er, Charity is . . . not well."

Albin looked at the preacher's face for a long moment and he asked the question Dolly didn't dare consider. "What did she mean—not well?"

The preacher cleared his throat and uncrossed and recrossed his long legs, straightening the crease in his trousers carefully.

"Out with it, man!" Albin's slow fuse was lit and, as always when it finally happened, could not be ignored.

"I'm sorry. But she says . . . there's an infant on the way."

Except for Dolly's convulsive swallow, silence reigned.

Finally Albin moved tiredly, "So—it's more serious than we thought."

"I would say so," the minister agreed. "Mrs. Murdoch said she can't have Charity working there much longer. She'll begin to . . . well, her pregnancy will show."

Dolly hid her face in her hands.

"And where is Gabriel Goss?" Albin, again, got to the root of the matter.

The preacher sighed. "Mrs. Murdoch doesn't know anything about him."

"Is Charity married?" Albin asked bluntly.

Rev. Victor spoke gently. "Mrs. Murdoch says she has a ring on her finger, but she doesn't think she's married."

O Lord . . . It was a prayer, not an expletive, that forced itself from Dolly's white lips. Modesty's eyes were suffused with tears.

"What can she be thinking of—not to come home?" Dolly cried. But under the gaze of the others, she added pitifully, "Surely she knows we love her."

"She won't come, Mum, I know it!" Modesty was positive.

"Oh, my poor child!"

The final blow had fallen; an illegitimate baby was the ultimate humiliation a family could face. A good, clean, honorable death could be faced more readily.

"In view of this new development," Gerald Victor said, "do you still want Charity here? Or shall we try and make some arrangement through Brother Higgins?"

Dolly reached through her tears for her husband's hand.

"We want her here," Albin said quietly. Modesty, sitting tensely, relaxed visibly.

"Well, then . . ." Again the minister seemed to hesitate.

And again Albin's jaw tightened.

Hastening on, Brother Victor said, "I have a suggestion I'd like you to consider. Obviously I'm not the one to bring her—she won't see me—and she absolutely refuses to see her family. There is, however, one person I believe Charity might talk to. And it may be the only one."

A slow flush crept up Dolly's neck, to erupt into an ugly stain when the minister finished simply: "Maggie."

In the silence that followed, Dolly's struggle was clear. It seemed an eternity before she said harshly, "Do what you think best."

"No—we'll do what *you* think best," her pastor said.

A cry escaped Dolly's lips. Getting to her feet in agitation, she walked to the window, pulled back the curtain, and stared out.

Finally, "Albin . . . ," she cried piteously.

"No, Mother, I'll not say it for you."

Whatever inner battle raged, it was over when Dolly turned. "I'll go to Maggie," she said. "I should have done so long ago."

"I'll go with you, if you like," volunteered the pastor.

"Or me," Albin added quickly.

"No, I need to do it, and I'll do it alone." With a return of her old spunk, Dolly added, "It's not going to seem as if someone dragged me over there—or like I was too weak-willed to do it alone."

The others smiled, relief on their faces; already Dolly moved and spoke with some of the old decisiveness.

To speak was to act with Dolly, and she put immediate action to her words. Changing her dress and straightening her hair, she marched out of the house, across the yard to the road, and turned in the direction of the Edwards farm.

No one ever knew for sure what further work went on in Dolly's heart on this walk, with the faithful Lord her only companion. But because of His faithfulness, her newly humbled spirit, and the powerfully present prayer of two old men—heads bowed at the side of their heater in their faded-green-door house across the district, never to know the full extent of their ministry until eternity revealed it—the face Dolly presented at the Edwardses' door was tear-stained, her eyes were puffed, and her usually tight-lipped mouth had softened and sweetened.

And no one ever knew what went on in Maggie's kitchen. Maggie never spoke of it except to say to her husband and son, "It's all right now, thank God!" Dolly never spoke of it.

But she returned with these words: "She'll go!" And fervently, "I bless her for it!"

And in a few days another drama unfolded, never to be revealed to outsiders, though much speculated about: Maggie delivered a pale and quiet Charity to her parents' home, turned her buggy, and drove away—but not before the door opened and arms reached out to the drooping figure standing on the step.

To John, Maggie confided, "Charity was desperate by the time I got there. She knew she couldn't keep that job there much longer; she wasn't well, and she had very little money—the job was little more than room and board.

"In Mrs. Murdoch's parlor the whole miserable story came out. Seemed like I just had to put my arms around her, and she broke . . . poor darling. I think she was glad to tell it, painful and sordid as it was.

"It seems, John, as if the day of the Sunday School picnic was more memorable than we knew."

In recalling that dramatic moment when Benjamin came back into her life, Maggie reminded them both of Charity's unexplained absence from most of the day's excitement, and Gabriel Goss's coinciding disappearance. "He apparently turned all his attention to her when Kate was out of reach. She was no match for his type of smooth operation. And innocent as she was, I guess she thought he was sincere."

"And, of course, she was in rebellion against Dolly's refusal to let her be with Marc," John interjected. "I never could understand that. Marc is a real man—sensible, industrious."

"Charity claims it's because his folks are Ukrainians . . . immigrants . . . from the old country! Weren't we *all* immigrants at one time? It's a wide and wonderful land—"

"And there's room for all of us."

"Well, whatever the reason, Dolly seems to have been the catalyst behind Charity's bid for independence. She was very angry at Marc, too—figured he should just ride away with her into the sunset in spite of her mother."

"Marc is too mature for that. He felt, I think, that it would all work out in time. He had definite plans."

"Anyway, Charity fell right in with Gabe's suggestion that they take off together, and they headed for Moose Jaw. They were married right away—I hope that part gets told when the rumors start to fly."

"They were married?" John's eyebrows lifted.

"The trouble was," Maggie's face hardened, "Gabriel Goss was already married. It wasn't too long until they ran across someone who knew him, and the fellow's confusion over Charity's name made her suspicious. Charity, as explosive as she is, got hysterical, packed her things in a rage, and left him. If she hadn't stumbled across Mrs. Murdoch—she went there to rent a room—no telling what might have happened to her.

"She soon knew she was pregnant. She confided in Mrs. Murdoch to a certain extent, and the rest you know—how Mrs. Murdoch talked with her pastor, how he wrote Brother Victor . . ."

"Poor Charity—a victim in more ways than one. What will happen to her now? People can be very cruel."

"As we know so well," Maggie murmured.

"Indeed we do. But out of it," and John reached a strong hand to his wife, "can come blessings."

"Treasures of darkness, and hidden riches of secret places," said the Sunday School teacher.

To all intents and purposes, life in Wildrose resumed its normal pattern, except that little was seen publicly of Charity Trimble. Dolly resumed her place at church, but with such a forbidding expression that no one dared ask a question or make a comment.

But in one small house—smelling of fresh-trimmed logs, almost barren of furnishings, and lonely beyond imagining—Marc Szarvas waged a bitter battle.

27

MARC DRIED THE WASHED AND RINSED SEPARA-
tor parts, reassembled them for use after the evening's
chores, and tossed the milky water from the steps. Chickens, those perennial optimists, came sprinting at the sound
to peck fruitlessly at the suds.

With morning chores, inside and out, completed, Marc
filled a basin with warm water from the reservoir of his
majestic range, stripped in its radiating heat, and bathed.

After toweling vigorously, he pulled on a newly ordered and just-received "fine finish, light-weight cham-
bray" shirt and dark union cassimere pants ("not too
heavy but that they can be worn at almost all seasons").
His springing hair yielded, at least for the moment, to vigorous brushing; the blade of a pocket knife dealt pitilessly
with his dirt-packed fingernails.

Wearing his best shoes and careful where he stepped,
he led the horse from the new barn and harnessed her to the
buggy. Tossing in a wool cardigan in case the day turned
cold, Marc jumped up onto the spring seat, picked up the
reins, and at a brisk trot turned the horse out of the yard to a
road from which the night's frost was melting, leaving it
black and damp. On this isolated road, his were the first
tracks of the day; perhaps they would be its only ones.

Before the bush hid it from sight, Marc looked back at
the neat, raw, log building he called home. Uncurtained

windows gleamed on each side of the well-hung door, a wisp of smoke drifted into the sky from the shiny stovepipe lifting above the low roof. A satisfying scene, in some ways.

But it was a shell, he thought honestly—just a shell, having never rung with song or laughter, never pulsated with emotions of love or vibrated with angry outcries. Childish voices had not impregnated its walls, nor the rasp of failing breath.

It was no stranger, however, to heavy sighs, lonely silences, and deep groanings. Always afterward, when morning dawned, emptiness returned, and the night's pain became another memory.

The long darknesses had been filled recently with something more; more than grief for things that might have been, things that never would be.

Marc, a farmer, had failed to count on the fact that dormant seeds, with or without encouragement, stir to life; from the dankest spot, tender sprouts spring forth because small, secret, hidden seeds cannot deny themselves.

How could he have forgotten? Why hadn't he counted on it, in the dark season of the soul?

When Marc first recognized that a persistent seed of love for Charity was not only sending forth a tendril from his blasted dreams but was firmly rooted and would not be dislodged, he had the courage to examine the phenomenon. For that's what it seemed to him to be, since it defied explanation.

But there it was: beneath the pain and the anger, the renunciation and the expulsion—a firmly implanted, death-defying root. Imbedded, twined around the very core of his being, it was bone of his bone and flesh of his flesh; it would die only when he died.

Marc painfully and honestly considered his alternatives. Without Charity he would live only half a life. And could he ever offer so little of himself to another woman?

But could he live with the evidence of Gabriel Goss's planting—already springing to life—always before him?

It was only when he knew he could that he laid aside forever, as an act of his will, the memory of his pain, picked up his abandoned dreams and plans, and rebuilt them to different specifications.

When Marc's buggy rattled into the Trimble yard, Charity, white-faced, ran to her room and dropped on the side of the bed. The faded cotton pinafore she wore thudded with the heavy beating of her heart as she listened for a clue to Marc's reason for coming; surely he would go on to the barn for some routine farm matter with her father.

But she heard the knock at the door and the muffled voices as her mother greeted him. The floor under her feet vibrated as footsteps crossed the kitchen floor to the front room to pause while a low conversation took place. Then Dolly's steps approached the bedroom door.

Charity looked up with apprehensive eyes as her mother closed the door, leaned against it, and said, "He wants to see you."

"No!"

"I think he means it."

"And I say no!"

Dolly was silent. Marc's purpose in coming had not been stated; he had simply asked to see Charity.

But Charity's refusal was adamant.

"Well," Dolly sighed, "I understand. Shall I ask him what he wants?"

"No . . . just ask him to go away. *Tell* him to go away."

Dolly stepped from the room, and Charity heard her footsteps take her to the man standing—waiting.

The footsteps that returned to the bedroom were heavy and purposeful, and Charity's hand flew to her throat. The door opened gently enough, however, and Marc stepped inside.

"Mum!" Harmony's eyes were round, her tone scandalized. *"Marc's going into Charity's bedroom!"*

"Don't worry about it."

"But Mum! What would good Queen Victoria say—"

"Don't be so concerned about what the queen says, child," Dolly said calmly. "Consider rather what the king says."

"The king?"

"King David. He said the steps of a good man are ordered by the Lord."

Harmony looked dazed.

"He also said," and Dolly's voice broke and her eyes misted, "'I was brought low, and he helped me.'"

"Who helped who?" Harmony was confused.

"Never mind. Run along and play. You're almost into your teen years, child; you'll be in Maggie Edwards' class soon—then you'll understand."

* * *

Behind the closed bedroom door, the face of the man who looked down upon her was empty of the expressions Charity had dreaded: anger, scorn, pity. Especially pity.

"I've asked your mother to leave us alone for a few minutes. I assured her that nothing . . . out of the way would go on."

A dull red flooded Charity's face. Her eyes dropped, and with an effort, not successful, she attempted to pull her stomach in by sitting up straight, loosening the binding of her pinafore around her swollen body.

When she raised her eyes, it was plain to see that Marc had taken in the whole fruitless endeavor.

At the misery in her eyes, his own flooded with compassion. There was only gentleness on his face as he sat down on the bed beside the trembling girl.

"Please," she whispered, "go away."

"Not until I say what's on my mind."

"Say it then, and go!" Charity spoke with a small show of her former spunk.

Marc smiled. It was going better than he had dared hope.

Marc was counting heavily on Charity's basic joy of life, her irrepressible personality, her natural resilience. Most of all he counted on her youth, trusting the recent experience, though sordid, might have touched her as lightly as possible and that, given an atmosphere free of blame and condemnation, her world would right itself and she would regain her buoyancy, becoming again the volatile, confident girl—woman—she had been.

Right now she seemed a child making a pathetic attempt at dignity. She leaned away from him, her chin lifted; but her eyes, hurt and defiant, reminded Marc of a coyote he had once caught in a trap. He wanted nothing more than to release her forever from the shame and pain he saw on her face by drawing her into the circle of his arms.

"Just let me talk," he began. "I've done a lot of thinking. I did a lot of hurting"—it was the only reference to his wounds he was to make—"and I've come to some conclusions. They're just about the same ones I had before."

Pain. Pain in her eyes, and he could have kicked himself.

"Cherry," the words came tumbling from him almost without thought, "I finished up the house . . . moved into it. I eat and sleep there. But it's nothing like I had dreamed. To me it's just a pile of logs.

"I have decided," he continued, watching her closely, "that I can either live in it like that for the rest of my life—lonely and empty—or I can do the thing I wanted to do all along."

Something flickered in Charity's eyes. Her hand went to her middle and her outstretched fingers covered the bulge pressing against her clothing.

Marc's eyes followed the gesture. "Would you trust

me . . . about all this?" he asked quietly, extending his rough hand and laying it, with warm pressure, over her own.

Now she was startled. "What—what do you mean?"

"I mean—it doesn't make any difference to me."

Knowing Charity well, Marc watched the play of emotions across her expressive face. She could so easily show disdain and anger, or be the outgoing, impulsively giving girl he had known.

"Can you believe that, Cherry?"

When she responded, it was not as angry child or impulsive girl. With new maturity and simple dignity she said, "I can believe it, Marc, because I've always believed you."

With that the dam broke. "And that was the trouble!" she continued. "I knew you meant what you said to Mum—about waiting! I knew you'd stick by your decision. It just made me feel so hopeless—and mad! I didn't want you to agree with Mum—to agree to wait!"

With astonishment Marc heard her out, his responsibility for the whole problem becoming clear for the first time: being so sure of his dreams and plans, he had ignored hers. His blindness, and her helplessness, had thrust them both into a pain they might have averted if he had taken a stand against Dolly and stood with Charity. Albin, he was sure, would have come around eventually.

Marc gathered Charity into his arms at last and, groaning, rocked her helplessly. "I'm sorry, Cherry . . . I'm sorry."

When the strong man's tears mingled with the deep sobs that poured from the girl with anger and frustration and humiliation, her mother, in the garden, heard, and covered her ears with her hands. Anyone watching would have sworn Dolly's twisted mouth moved in a prayer that seemed suspiciously like, *O God! Forgive me!*

And then—except for the weeds Dolly yanked and

tossed into a pile, the distant sounds of Albin's activities, and a small girl's hum as she pumped herself into the biting air on a swing under the poplar tree at the garden's edge—silence prevailed.

When the screen door slammed, Dolly looked up. Charity, apron removed, with a coat over her shoulders and an old fascinator over her head, stepped onto the porch, Marc at her side. Side by side they walked across the yard, past the shed and the forge, through the gate, and into the meadow beyond. Soon the bush hid them from sight.

Only then did Dolly's clenched hands relax their grip on the dry tomato plant she was clutching. Gently she laid it on top of the pile.

When Charity and Marc returned they were hand in hand; Charity's eyes were washed empty of tears, and a glimmer of hope and happiness shone there.

Pulling the buggy into the yard after a trip to Meridian for mail and supplies, Modesty was startled to see Marc Szarvas's horse and buggy. Hastily filling her arms with her purchases, she hurried into the house to find Marc and Charity talking seriously with her father and mother—about marriage.

Marc's arm was around Charity's thickening waist in a possessive manner. "Modesty," he said, to her astonishment, "Cherry and I are going to do what we should have done a long time ago," and Dolly, looking disconcerted, didn't challenge the logic.

"Cherry's going to marry me," Marc said with a grin. "Come and greet your brother-in-law to be!"

"I was willing to wait until after the baby comes," Charity told her sister later in the privacy of the bed they shared. "Somehow I thought it might seem more . . . decent. But Marc won't have it that way. He says"—Charity's voice shook—"'This baby is going to be born with a name'—and it's going to be *his* name."

"Szarvas." Modesty's tone was wry. "Poor Mum—I bet she doesn't know whether to bless or to burn the *immigrant* name of her first grandchild!"

"Sometimes, Moddy," Charity said, voice thick, "I wonder if I'll ever forgive her."

"Try, Charity," her sister encouraged. "She's suffered too. She needs your forgiveness. But more: you need what it will do for you—and the baby."

Charity grunted, and then silence reigned as sleep drifted over the sisters with a peace they hadn't known in a long time.

"Moddy," Charity said at last, "I'm not marrying Marc as a last resort or because I'm desperate, though God knows I've been that. I've loved him for a long time. I'll make him a good wife; I know I will."

Modesty squeezed her sister's hand, and hand in hand they fell asleep.

* * *

The wedding was simple. Marc and Charity had offered to go to Prince Albert or to the Victor parsonage, but Albin was firm and Dolly agreed: Charity would be married in her own home and her father would give her away.

If the new dress was designed to be let out in the seams later on, who could tell? If the bride's trousseau included flannel napkins, bellybands, and tiny embroidered sacques, who knew but the sister who had so lovingly worked away at them when the mother-to-be had lain in quiet despair in a darkened bedroom?

And if the silence that fell when the preacher intoned, "If anyone knows just cause why this man and this woman should not be united in matrimony, let him now speak or else forever hold his peace," was broken by the sound of the bride's indrawn breath, it returned to normal when the sturdy groom at her side reached out—no matter that it was at the wrong moment in the ceremony—and took her trembling hand in his.

Aside from the two families and the preacher, one other person attended: Maggie Edwards was welcomed at the door with a kiss from the teary-eyed bride, a warm hug from the contented groom, and a heartfelt embrace from a humble-eyed Dolly.

After the ceremony and the refreshments that followed, Marc tucked his bride into his buggy, surrounded by the remainder of her possessions (a wagonload had been taken over to her new home a few days previously and put in place), and the newlyweds waved good-bye to the loved ones huddled in the cold on the porch, drove out of the Trimble yard, down the road, and over the small hills of the bush country toward the empty, waiting cabin.

Billy, Marc's young brother, had hurried on ahead through the twilight and had the house warm for them. He waited until the buggy creaked up to the door, helped carry the boxes and bags inside, then, with a grin, he bowed out of the door and slipped away to care for Marc's horse before riding home.

Marc closed the door behind his brother. Lifting the coat from Charity's shoulders, he hung it on the hook he had arranged for that purpose. He took the lamp from its place on the shelf, lit it, and placed it in the center of his table. He looked around at the simple furnishings, the sturdy log walls, the crackling fire, and the girl of his dreams, the center of it all at last.

Somehow it didn't seem too fanciful, in that moment, to feel that happiness had come home.

Putting his hands on Charity's shoulders, Marc tipped her face up to his and looked long into her eyes, from which all teasing had fled (but, pray God, not forever). What he saw there was enough to carry him through the night, the next strange months, the stretching years.

 **28**

"UPON THE LAND OF MY PEOPLE SHALL COME UP thorns and briers; yea, upon all the houses of joy in the joyous city," the preacher read.

The scripture, so like the one Trapper Farley had quoted to Linn on threshing day, fell on her ears like a voice crying in the wilderness of her emptiness and hopelessness.

Her attention had been fixed blindly on the bare tree branches visible through the schoolhouse windows rather than on the man in the rusty suit behind the pulpit/desk. But at the scripture reading, she turned her thoughts from the approaching dreary winter to what she expected would be an equally dreary word from the pulpit—and found it a word from God.

The message Brother Victor brought was rich in an imagery they all understood as he compared a weed-choked field to a care-choked heart.

"The problem," he said, "is in the seed that is sown. Many people, eager for a harvest of happiness, reap scantily if at all, having sown the seeds of discontent.

"Happiness," the man of God explained, "is a byproduct. Joy is a fruit. The proper seed, planted and cultivated in the human heart, will blossom into a harvest of joy. Then, even though happiness, based on circumstances and conditions, should disappear, the soul's joy remains.

"Happiness, as I see it," he said with a smile to people well familiar with seedtime and harvest, "is an annual. Joy is a perennial and will survive the harshest winters to flourish again."

The simple lesson continued. Linn, with her first glimmer of a better day—a better way—felt a small thrill in the wastelands of her heart, as though a tendril had stirred tentatively. Joy, she dared believe, would follow in its season.

"Let the Master Gardener do His cultivating," the preacher urged. "Submit to His pruning, and expect the fruit of His Spirit in bountiful harvest."

It was a thoughtful Linn who turned her steps down the hill homeward.

As though her eyes had been opened, she noted how the riotous growth of the bush was laced with thistles, weeds, and nettles. But here and there the sturdy wild rose did battle for its place in the sun. There was no evidence now of the rampant blooms and their recent beauty and fragrance.

But they would blossom again! In spite of the weeds' tenacious grip and winter's harshest weather, the wild rose was rooted and grounded in good parkland soil, and in its season it would bloom again.

If Celia noted her daughter's preoccupation, she was wise enough not to comment on it as they ate their light Sunday noon meal, cleared away the dishes and food, and went their separate ways—Celia and Judd to needed rest, Linn to wander the much-loved and familiar paths of farmyard, field, and bush.

Finally, in a sheltered corner, a wisp of color lifted bravely toward the last touches of the sun's warmth, and Linn turned aside and made her way to it through the tangle of brambles.

Remembering that Trapper Farley had shared spring's first crocus with her, Linn found herself wishing he were there to share summer's last rose.

But Trapp was gone from her life. Not, however, before he had exposed, gently but unmistakably, the condition of her heart. "Made for crocuses and roses," he had said, ". . . overgrown with thorns."

"I need," Linn had the insight to see and the courage to say, "a place in the Son."

*　*　*

Evening's shadows were falling when, following supper, Linn turned her steps, deliberately and finally, up the hill.

The small building, etched now against the sunset sky, was the only church she knew, a rustic cathedral in the heart of the bush. In it she had been taught the simple gospel message. It held the only altar available to her—a rude bench. Opening the door, she stepped over the threshold and into the silent shadows.

Making her way with sure steps through the familiar maze of desks, Linn passed the battered pulpit to the rude bench—a mourner's bench, some called it. Here she knelt, and her broken prayer was the surrender of a life tired of its own way. The tears that splashed onto the bench's worn surface were an outward sign of the cleansing of a repentant heart as it acknowledged its selfishness and yielded its stubbornness to the better ways of a much higher, wiser Power and found forgiveness.

It did not take long. She had, after all, come to the One who had invited, "Come unto me," and who had promised, "I will give you rest."

The arms that reached for Linn were almighty arms; the love that enfolded her was everlasting. And the peace, the blessed peace, was past all understanding.

And when she rose from her knees, it was with the satisfying and heartwarming assurance that, indeed, "old things are passed away . . . all things are become new."

Turning to the little room, Linn found it cleansed of bitter memories; they had taken flight as swiftly and easily as the troubled day was fading into peaceful twilight. The evening's first star, glinting through the tall windows, was no brighter than the tears that stung her eyes afresh, pain's final rinse and freedom's release.

Linn closed the door on the past, and as she stepped out into the clean, sweet Wildrose twilight, she felt she moved into a clean and sweet realm of the Spirit.

29

SOMEHOW ON THIS NIGHT LINN WAS NOT SUR-
prised to hear a nicker and to see, in the night's early
darkness, a familiar figure—lithe, leanly muscled, vigorous—leaning on the schoolhouse fence, a horse tethered
beside him.

And somehow it seemed natural to move alongside
and lean her arms, as he was doing, on the top rail.

Trapper Farley was engrossed, it seemed, in a study of
the sky.

Finally, in the comfortable silence, Linn—now stargaz-
ing as studiously as he—said hesitantly, "I was in the—the
church." For some reason, she could not call it a schoolhouse tonight.

"I know."

In the silence that followed, a night creature rustled
the nearby bush. It, too, silenced with the stamping of the
horse's hoof.

In a low voice, Linn began. "In there," and her head
tipped toward the small building, "I did a little praying—
and a lot of thinking. Things—certain things—fell into
place . . . at last." Her voice was hesitant, her words groping.

Trapp waited.

Linn drew a quivering breath. "I don't know why I

didn't do it before. I guess . . . I suppose I wasn't ready to let the Lord—" She paused.

"Clear out the thistles and nettles?" Trapp finished quietly for her.

"That's it," she admitted. "And now—now I feel so much better. It's like everything's new, Trapp—a new beginning."

"Like spring."

"Like spring in the bush," said the girl who loved it to one who was learning to. "Spring in the bush, and a fresh start."

The silence was peaceful.

"And, Trapp, I need—I need to ask you to forgive me."

"Forgive you, Linn?"

"For my harshness—my unkindness; I had no right," Linn said painfully, "to accuse you . . ." Again she paused.

"Accuse me?"

"That day at the picnic. But I had been badly humiliated once—you know, when Abram . . . and when another man came along and another situation that seemed to be like the first one, I lashed out. It was unfair—I see that now.

"You have a right to your own life, Trapp. I had no reason to—" Linn's voice, in spite of herself, thickened. With an effort she continued, "I'm so sorry."

Here her voice broke. She dropped her head onto her arms on the fence rail. "I'm sorry, Trapp," she whispered. "Please forgive me."

"Let's just forget it," Trapper Farley said quietly and turned again to contemplation of the heavens.

The moon, its wick lit, was slowly burning brighter and brighter, muting the dead and dying bush and touching the whole world with a pearly sheen.

The rattle of the horse's bridle as the mare blew softly and tossed her head was the only sound to fill the starry night.

"And, Trapp," Linn said finally, her voice muffled but determined, her eyes fixed on the horse rather than the man, "I sincerely wish you and Berry the very best. I hope—I'm sure you'll be very happy."

"Thanks," Trapp said mildly. "I hope you include Boyd."

"Boyd?" Linn turned her head at last and looked at Trapper Farley; why should he bring his cousin into this?

"If Berry is happy," Trapp said matter-of-factly, "I'm sure it will make Boyd happy."

Linn stared fixedly, for a long moment, at Trapp's profile. "Make . . . Boyd . . . happy?"

"He loves her very much."

Silence. Thick silence.

"Boyd . . . and Berry?" Linn repeated stupidly.

"Always!" Trapp answered promptly.

When his meaning penetrated, Linn grasped the fence rail to keep from swaying. And the awareness of how unfair, how very unfair, she had been to this man, how wrong, how accusing and all without basis, it threatened to overwhelm her—except for Trapp's laughter. Tremulously, Linn joined in.

"Berry . . . and Boyd!" she said unbelievingly.

"Berry and Boyd," he agreed.

Linn loosed her grip of the railing to turn, full face, to look directly at Trapper Farley. "Oh, Trapp!" she breathed. "Does this mean you'll be staying in Wildrose?"

"Always!" he said again.

Overhead a ragged formation regrouped as wild geese played follow the leader across the sky, calling in the night. Trapp and Linn watched as the graceful phalanx swept out of the dark, to be outlined momentarily against the brilliant orb of the moon before winging soundlessly southward.

"They'll be back," Trapp said, and it sounded like a promise. "Come spring, they'll be back."

And Linn knew she could count on it.